Also by Kathi Reed

Banking on Trouble

Trouble For Rent

TROUBLE

IN WONDERLAND

an Annie Fillmore mystery

KATHI REED

For David and Stephanie.
I couldn't have invented better children.

TABLE OF CONTENTS

PROLOGUE

Why do murders seem to follow me like a bad smell? Or do I follow them? Either way I can't seem to dodge it. The video convention in Kentucky where I was supposed to learn things about building my business stank to high heaven. You know how water smells after dead flowers have befouled it for about a week? Kind of like that.

I'm Annie Fillmore, owner of Annie's Video and Music Hall in Briartown, Ohio. I purchase my videos from Wonderly Entertainment in Wonderly, Kentucky—about two hours south of my store, across the Ohio River from Cincinnati.

One fateful day in September, I opened an envelope from Wonderly Entertainment in which I found this:

WONDERLY ENTERTAINMENT

INVITES YOU TO

HOLLYWOOD IN KENTUCKY

OCTOBER 18-20, 1991

⬩MEET THE STARS

⬩MINGLE WITH YOUR PEERS

⬩LET THE EXPERTS TEACH YOU

HOW TO MAKE MORE $$$

*PRIZES, FREEBIES

*SHOP OUR WAREHOUSE FOR THOU-
SANDS OF SALE VIDEOS

Leaving my livelihood for three days didn't sound like something I could pull off. I would usually consider myself lucky if I even got a Sunday free. But the prospect of discount videos, not to mention what I might learn from the so-called experts, convinced me that my employees and friends Marilyn, Neil, Kelly, and Josh could keep the store afloat while I was away. I decided to do it. I'd leave my happy routine behind for a few days and, like Daniel Boone (sans the coonskin cap), sally forth into Kentucky. But Daniel may have fared better than I did when all was said and done. I wouldn't be fighting off the Shawnee, but at least he knew who his enemies were.

Why my life takes on a hint of the malodorous is anybody's guess. My Moms' guess is that I draw it to me. Seriously? Who wants to attract that kind of stench? I must be some messed-up chick.

CHAPTER 1

"Meet the stars? That sounds a bit of all right," Neil said, leaning over my shoulder to read the announcement. He might not admit it, but I've learned that Neil is a devotee of fame. He also favors speaking in Britishisms, no doubt a result of his love of Second British Invasion groups. One of his favorites is The Pogues, who he repeatedly informs me are actually English Celtic punk. All I knew was I liked their music even if the lead guy had rotting teeth.

"Hmm I wonder what kind of Hollywood stars are going to a convention in Kentucky?" I asked rhetorically.

"Maybe Rosanna Arquette?" Neil asked hopefully.

"I doubt it. She's not in a movie that's being released in November or December. I'm pretty sure if there are stars attending they'll be promoting their movies that are coming out soon."

"You've just burst my celebrity balloon," said Neil, feigning disappointment.

"And anyway, you're not going. I'm going, and I don't care if Rosanna Arquette is there or not. Maybe Kurt Russell, though. It would be nice to meet him."

"What's so hot about Kurt Russell?" Neil said.

Was he serious? Or was he jealous? After knowing him for almost a year, our relationship had become complex. I had a dream about us one night that we were competing rug merchants in Marrakech yelling and shaking fists. The whole shebang. I've never even been to Marrakech. I wasn't surprised that my Moms said it was a dream about a past life. We weren't competing in this life though, unless it was for my heart, which I was attempting to hang onto tooth and nail.

Neil Jakhaar is the music buyer at my store, a job he prefers to his other job at his uncle's business, Choice Travel Agency. Despite the twenty-year disparity in our ages (he's the younger), there was an attraction I couldn't seem to shake even though I desperately wanted to.

"Can't I go? Seriously?" he begged.

"Who's going to watch the store? You're my number-one backup. If you go, I can't go," I said.

"Bummer," he said resignedly. "Yeah, I have to be at the travel agency, anyway. There goes my brush with fame.

"I'll get autographs if there are any to get," I cajoled.

The doorbell jangled, and we both looked up.

"What are you two video gangsters up to?" asked Marilyn as she lumbered across the floor toward us. The baby carrier strapped to her chest looked way too weighty. She was kind of stooped over.

Marilyn Monroe (née Klotzman) was my best friend since the day she walked into my store and introduced herself. That's all it took. She has three boys; Jackson, Andrew, and Norman who are six, four, and eighteen months, respectively. Her husband, Tom, is allegedly distantly related to Andrew Jackson, thus their eldest sons' names. Too bad he wasn't related to Abraham Lincoln. Wanting to assert her own quasi heritage, Marilyn named Norman after her famous Hollywood namesake.

Despite her perpetual state of fatigue, she helps out at Annie's on Monday nights as a respite from her demanding brood. This escape is made possible by Tom's mother, Katy, who jumps at the chance to spend time with her grandkids.

"Do you think Norman might be too heavy for that thing?" I proposed.

"He's too heavy for Arnold Schwarzenegger. But it's either this or get the stroller into the car, haul it out of the car, then get *him* out of the car, then… It's exhausting. It's a toss-up between a broken back and fainting in the parking lot."

"Well he looks happy," I said.

"God only knows why. He doesn't sleep worth a damn. Is he sleeping now?" she asked.

"Yep, down and out," I reported.

"If he doesn't sleep, I don't sleep. But he gets to sleep during the day. How unfair is that?"

"He *is* the baby," I pointed out.

"Enough about sleepless babies and their overwhelmed mothers. I feel like I'm juggling ten flaming torches even though my hands are only big enough for five. What's going on with you?"

"Hey," Neil interrupted, "I gotta get going. Bye Norm…bye girls," he said as he walked out the door in his long black coat from Goodwill. He cut an unusual figure with that coat, what he calls his black trainers, and his black backpack. One of my customers, after meeting him, asked me if I were helping out a homeless person.

"I just received this invite from Wonderly Entertainment to go to their yearly convention. I haven't gone before, but I think I'll give it a try. Just the thought of leaving the store for three days has me feeling wobbly—like drunken wobbly," I said to Marilyn.

"It'll be fine. I can be around more now that these titties are safely back in my regular bra. The one without trap doors. And, besides, Neil will be here whenever I need him...and, of course, Kelly and Josh. You know, I should hand over my three to one of their parents. They both turned out pretty well."

Kelly Heitz and Josh Roberts were high school kids who made life at the store easier. You always hear about teenage kids having no sense of responsibility. I know I didn't when I was seventeen. But these two conduct themselves as if they were years older. They're punctual, helpful, and respectful. They deserve more then I'm paying them. Alas.

"Ha. You know how kids are always great when they're not home," I mused.

"I just stopped in to say hi and to get a break. Katy's home with Andrew and Jackson, so I'd better get back. Home is where the mess is. Have you heard that expression? No? I just made it up."

And off she went.

Posters needed to come down and go up. I eyed the summer posters that had been on the walls for a while: *Edward Scissorhands, Goodfellas, L.A. Story.* September is a slow month for videos stores, with kids back to school and sports starting back up. I have to be creative with how I place posters. Popular posters such as *Backdraft, Fantasia,* and *What About Bob?* have to go up even if it would be a month or more until those videos actually made it to the store.

At the end of August I received a delightful promotional blow-up Prancer for advertising an upcoming release of a holiday movie called just that, Prancer. It had been in place only a week but it got a lot of attention from both the kids and their parents.

Everyone likes a Christmas movie—even if it's advertised in September. I knew it was popular when people asked me to reserve the video when it came in—November 8. Usually promotions are key chains, koozies, playing cards, little flashlights, plastic cups. All with the name of the movie they're advertising emblazoned on them. Prancer put those little doodads to shame and was already reaping benefits.

I was balancing on top of a ladder to get *Backdraft* in the spotlight position when I heard the doorbell jingle.

"Don't move, Annie. Just dropping off and looking for something I haven't seen," said the woman with the gravelly voice that I recognized without even turning around.

"Hey, Nan. I'll be right down."

"Take your time. I know the lay of the land," she rasped.

Nan Lewis was a "lifer," or someone who rented movies two to three times a week. What a charmer. On top of that gold star next to her name she was just plain delightful. She adored her three small children, and, unlike so many of us, thought all of life was just a bowl of cherries.

The door opened again as I was getting down from the ladder and three teen-age boys came in.

"Hi guys" Nan greeted them before I did. "What are you doing on this side of town, Dylan?" she asked.

He mumbled, "Just hanging out with my friends."

I hadn't seen these particular kids before and something looked off. They didn't go to the music section as do most kids in the afternoon; they kind of roamed around by the Children's section which was odd. But I paid it no more attention once I got busy with checking Nan out with *My Left Foot* and *National Lampoon's Christmas Vacation*.

"I know you've seen *Christmas Vacation* before," I said.

"Oh yeah, about five times. But it's a family favorite. We laugh just as much every time. 'Can I refill your eggnog? Get you something to eat, drive you into the middle of nowhere, and leave you for dead?' That kills us every time," she chortled.

Just as we were laughing, the three boys hot-footed it out of the store.

"What's up with them?" I asked, and turned to where they had come from.

"Oh, my God, they've killed Prancer," I moaned. There was what looked like a cigarette hole in Prancer's chest, and he was gracefully falling to the ground in a heap of tan plastic.

"Can you stay here a minute, Nan? I'm going after those creeps."

I grabbed the limp Prancer and dragged him out the front door into the parking lot. They had backed into their space, presumably with the idea of making a quick getaway. I held up the pathetic wad of plastic and yelled through the windshield at them, "You've killed Prancer!"

Shoppers stopped their carts, gawking and wondering, no doubt, what the hell I was screaming about.

The hoodlums looked astonished at first, then started to laugh. It was at that point that I remember feeling like my hair had spontaneously combusted. Oooh, was I pissed!

"Laugh now you little shits. I know your names, and I'm calling your parents to let them know what their darling sons have been up to. This is how mass murderers start out." What's beyond pissed? That's what I was.

As soon as I was back in the store, Nan asked, "What did they do?"

When I told her, she said, "I'm sure their parents don't know they smoke. Dylan comes from a nice family."

"So did Jack the Ripper," I said. "I'm sorry, Nan. I don't mean to be crazy, but that's so unnecessary. If my kids did that, I'd be furious. Wouldn't you?"

"Oh yeah. Mine wouldn't see the light of day until Christmas," she said obligingly.

And so it goes in the life of a video store owner; at least *this* video store owner.

I put all that crapola behind me while getting ready to devote three whole days to a convention. Normal people would do less to prepare for a trip around the world. Clothing choices alone took a good bit of time. I wondered what people would wear to a video convention in Kentucky? Buckskin? Petticoats? Or, I thought, maybe I should go the horse-country route: jodhpurs, riding boots, crops? I'm only half kidding when I say that these thoughts crossed my mind. In the end I finally decided to wear what I usually wear. Black. Because this is what is hanging in my closet. I did buy a few non-black items to perk up the funereal ensembles. And so that I would not be mistaken for Neil.

Figuring out the schedule, back-up, and the back-up to back-up schedule took up much of the rest of the month.

"We've got it covered," and "Don't worry about it," didn't cut it. I wanted the type of guarantee that doesn't exist. But that store was my life: my financial security, my social life, and my love life all rolled into one. If anything bad were to happen, what the hell would I have done? Gotten a job? Nah.

One night my buddy, Sophie Sugarman, helped me out when I was working alone. She happened to come in to rent a video while the place was hopping and ended up sliding behind the counter as if she'd worked her whole life in a video store. So I enlisted her to share her phone number with Neil, just in case.

My worries were somewhat assuaged after Sophie volunteered to be on call. Until my Moms phoned.

My two Moms, Helen and Emilie (actually my maternal and paternal aunts who adopted me just after my parents died when I was a baby) are metaphysical wizards. It would be an exaggeration to say they know when I have one hair out of place, but not hyperbole to say they know when I'm leaving town. They seem to know what lurks around every corner, especially if it's danger. Especially if it's *my* corner.

"Are you planning a trip, dear?" asked Helen.

"I guess you know I am, right? Some goblin whispered in your ear that I was going to a video convention in Kentucky?"

"We didn't know it was a video convention, but we do see a lot of grey aura surrounding you," chirped Helen, ignoring my goblin reference.

"Is the grey surrounding me or the store?" I asked, heart pounding. When you care more about the well-being of your business than you do about your own personal security, you must have a screw loose.

"Oh no, dear, we can't know anything about inanimate objects, just human beings and animals, naturally."

Naturally, I thought.

She continued, "We want you to be aware of your surroundings and especially any bad vibes you might feel about people."

"Not animals? What if I come upon a bear in the woods?"

"Now you're being silly, there are no bears where you're going, I'm sure of that," Helen said, chuckling. "Em would like to have a word, too, Annie. I love you. Be careful."

"Annie, my dear, it might be a good idea to take that little gun along on the trip," Em suggested.

During a visit from Helen and Em, one of my crazed customers thought it would be a great idea to shoot me, and I found out then that Em was a sharpshooter, knew all about guns, and felt carrying a gun was as natural as carrying an extra set of keys.

"I don't think so, Mom. I wouldn't feel comfortable."

"You'll feel less comfortable if someone comes into your room at night to steal something or to do you harm and you're unprotected. I'm telling you this because we are sensing some kind of danger. We love you. We surely do not want you to come to any harm in Kentucky."

Em was all business. She said flat out they sensed danger, while Helen was more circumspect and told me they saw me surrounded by some kind of grey fog. My natural habitat, actually.

"I'll think about it," I mumbled. "I love you both, and I'll talk to you when I get back," I said, sounding less forlorn than I felt.

That was a chipper phone call. It sounded like I'd be heading for a world of trouble in Kentucky.

CHAPTER 2

Driving over the Ohio River on the Brent Spence Bridge, which connects Ohio to Kentucky, I heard in my head, "Trucks to the left of me, trucks to the right of me, here I am stuck in the middle with you." Well, there was no *you*, but there sure were a lot of trucks. Smooshed between two semis, all I could see were more trucks. And their nauseating exhaust fumes seeped into my little Honda. The cantilevered bridge looked like it was made from an Erector set. That alone didn't give me confidence that halfway over I wasn't going to fall into the brown flowing river, never mind the trucks.

I was accustomed to the route up until I got off on I-275 toward the Cincinnati/Northern Kentucky International Airport, but was hoping after that I'd see some of the beautiful state of Kentucky. I did have to get past the red-and-white-striped water tower that announced Florence Y'all, which, originally, was meant to advertise Florence Mall, but legal considerations made that impossible, so they changed it to what it is, Y'all. You have to love Kentucky.

As I drove farther into Kentucky, the clouds settled on the horizon looking like blowsy grey mountains. The rolling hills and green forests on either side of me were a welcome change to the ominous tractor trailers.

Surprisingly, autumn colors had not arrived as they had in Ohio. Some of the trees had started to turn red and gold, but just.

When I exited the interstate, the world changed. The wide, flat highway gave way to narrow, winding roads lined with dilapidated tobacco barns. Small towns with general stores popped up without notice. Double-wide trailers appeared along the side of the road complete with broken cars on blocks in their front yards. And rolling hills topped with farm-houses set a bucolic scene.

The directions I received with the invitation got me to Wonderly in less time than I thought it would, though I did have my pedal to the metal. Arriving in town, my heart skipped a beat. I was always a sucker for an adventure, no matter how small.

I drove to The Dunbar, the hotel where I and, I assumed, all the other video store owners would be staying. At first glance, it didn't look too inviting. An eight-story rectangle of brick, the hotel was surrounded by parking lots. So much for my bucolic reverie. Added to my dismay, it struck me at that moment that the owner of Wonderly Entertainment was named Dunbar and had likely named this penitentiary of a hotel after himself. I wasn't beguiled.

Wheeling my small suitcase through the front doors adorned on either side with **WELCOME TO WONDERLY** signs, I found myself in the midst of a hive of people.

The check-in line was long, so when I took my place I took the opportunity to explore the lobby. And by "explore the lobby," I mean check out the other attendees. A woman standing behind me tapped me on the shoulder and asked, "Are you somebody, or do you just own a video store?"

I turned around to find that my questioner had curly red hair, painted-on eyebrows, lips like Betty Boop, and enough nugget jewelry to open a pawnshop.

"I'm somebody *and* I own a video store." What did she mean?

"Oh, I'm Daisy Dixon. We own Video Vixen in Covington, Kentucky, ya know. I thought you might be a celebrity. You kinda dress like that Diane Keaton; she dresses plain like you."

I was wearing black pants, a black shirt, and red Doc Martens on my feet.

She smiled at me. Even though I guess it was an insult, I felt kind of cool being compared to Diane Keaton. I love Diane Keaton.

"Hermy, Hermy," Daisy called out, waving her hands skittishly, almost slapping people who stood too close to her windmill arms. "Over here."

Hermy was lumbering toward us, dragging two big bellman's carts full of clothing bags and suitcases. The obedient husband, I presumed.

"Are you staying longer than three days?" I asked.

"We never know. You brought extra suitcases for the free stuff, didn't you?" Daisy asked

"Uh, no. What free stuff?"

"The studio giveaways. They give them to us to promote their movies, but we stick a price tag on them and sell them. You sell everything, don't you know that?"

"Uh, no." I was quite the conversationalist.

"Who's your rep? Didn't he tell you?" Daisy asked quizzically.

"Rob Woodbury," I answered.

"He's our rep, too. I guess it slipped his mind to tell you to bring more suitcases for the loot."

"Hmm," I answered. Rob Woodbury didn't seem like the kind of guy who would tell me to bring a satchel to bring home booty the studios were giving away.

I tried valiantly at that point to introduce myself, but she kept talking. About something. But finally I got an opening.

"By the way, I'm Annie Fillmore. I own Annie's Video and Music Hall in Briartown, Ohio," I barged in.

"We thought of buying another store up there, but it's way too small a town for the kind of video store we like," she said smugly. "Oh, and have you met Dun Wonderly yet?" Daisy asked with what seemed like stars in her eyes.

"The guy who owns Wonderly Entertainment? No."

"Oh, just you wait. He not only owns the video wholesale part of this, he owns the hotel—and the distillery next door. He owns everything. He's really rich. What a catch," Daisy said, beaming with delight, arching her already impossibly arched eyebrows.

"Annie. Annie Fillmore," I heard as I was attempting to tear my eyes away from Daisy's brows, trying to decide if they were drawn on or tattooed.

"Hi, Rob. Great to see you. This place is hopping." I said, looking around again at the bustling crowd waiting to register.

"I'll wait for you while you register and I greet customers. Just keep your eye out for me and I'll let you know what's next, or you can rest a bit before the evening's activities."

"Oh, hey, wait a minute," he said. "I guess you haven't met Dun Wonderly yet? He's over there talking to one of the Disney reps. I'll introduce you."

Watching him make his way to where two men were standing and talking to the Disney guy, I realized how tall Rob was and how he was the perfect stereotype of a mid-western dad: khaki pants, plaid madras shirt, brown hush puppies, clipped brown hair styled with a side part, and all of it without a wrinkle.

Mr. Disney looked like Hollywood to me with his short salt-and-pepper hair, John Lennon glasses, and bespoke tweed jacket. At least, I thought he was Disney. I figured that the older man with him was Mr. Wonderly. I wasn't sure about the other guy. He was shorter, had Rob's hairdo in blond, and was wearing a T-shirt and khakis.

Rob led two gentlemen over to where I was standing.

"Dun Wonderly, let me introduce Annie Fillmore of Annie's Video and Music Hall," Rob said with his arm around Dun's shoulder.

Dun sized me up and seemed to dismiss me in less than three seconds. It took less than that for me to dismiss him. He was tall, probably about six feet, and his dyed light brown hair was combed over to hide his freckled pate, which it didn't quite do. His gibbous moon-shaped stomach flopped over the top of his sans-a-belt pants, testing the elasticity of his blue button-down shirt.

"Pleased to meet ya. Ya not from these parts Robbie tells me."

"No, I live in Cincinnati," I said.

"Well, that's still kinda these parts. I mean you weren't born in this neck of the woods?"

"No, I'm from New York City."

"Well, wadda ya know. Are you a Jew?"

I gasped. Rob looked down, shaking his head. Only the other guy standing there smiled engagingly.

"No, sir. My religion is courtesy and love of my fellow man." I might have stretched the point with courtesy because I was desperately trying not to call him an asshole.

"Still could be a Jew," he said chuckling. "Heh heh."

Oh, my God. Yahweh or otherwise, I thought.

"Let me introduce you to Bucky," Rob said, attempting to stem the flow of vitriol he must have perceived gushing out of my ears. "Bucky, Annie Fillmore. Annie's store is in northern Cincinnati, in Briartown."

"Hey! How you doing?" Bucky said, winking at me. "It's great to meet all our customers face- to-face. I'm Dun's right-hand man. So if you need anything that Rob can't help you with, you call on me. Okay? I mean that sincerely," he said. His smile wrapped around his face so far it was literally ear-to-ear. He was short and wiry unlike his portly boss. His bright blue T-shirt said Welcome to Wonderly in the same font as the door signs but with a little cartoon in a speech bubble underneath saying, "We Love Our Customers." It was smartly tucked into his well-fitting tan canvas pants.

"Heh heh heh, my right hand is a lot smarter than Bucky. Am I right or am I right, Buck?" joshed Dun.

"Nice to meet you, Bucky," I responded.

"Dun, Dun," I heard from behind.

"Well, hail, I was lookin' for you. The Dixon Vixen, one of my favorite customers," said Dun, throwing his arms around Daisy.

"Dun, you old dog. I just couldn't wait to get down here and see your handsome face," Daisy gushed.

Handsome face? I turned to look a little closer to see what she thought was handsome. The hangdog jowls, obviously false pearly whites, the gibbous moon?

"Now that the vixen's here, the party can get started," he said, still with his arm around her, now at her waist.

I was just waiting for him to make his way down to her ass.

"Hermy, say hi to Dun," Daisy said, pulling Hermy forward by his arm.

"Well, shee-it, I always do forget you're married," Dun chuckled.

"Nice to see you, too," Hermy said sarcastically.

"Heh heh heh."

"May I help you, ma'am?"

I turned around to find a lovely young woman standing behind the registration desk. My vexing introduction to Dun Wonderly had me seeing red, and I didn't realize I had been right in front of the counter. JESSICA read the name tag of the comely receptionist.

"Oh, sorry. Yes, I'm Annie Fillmore. I have a reservation."

"Welcome to The Dunbar," she said with a sweet smile and handed me a large key to room 237.

I looked around for Rob, who had moved on to a circle of five women apparently in cordial conversation. I'd catch him later.

Making my way out of the throng with my suitcase on the little luggage wheels, I noticed that the burgundy patterned carpet was threadbare in places, and looking up, that the cream walls needed a good scrubbing or, better yet, repainting. Over my right shoulder a glass elevator ascended, crammed with conventioneers looking a little like my overstuffed Adventure section. I wondered about the capacity of the elevator. Then I wondered how long it would take it to plummet to the lobby. But as I watched with quasi-dread, I realized that there was a moving object among the elevator sardines and that the thing moving was Daisy Dixon waving at me excitedly. I took the stairs.

Fantasizing that my bright red suitcase was a mere feather, I struggled with the flimsy metal luggage carrier on the stairs, swearing under my breath until the first landing. The elastic cord that was supposed to keep my suitcase in place had worked its way off. Screw it, I thought. I lifted the whole damn thing and carried it up the last set of stairs.

Directly in front of me at the top of the stairs was a little plaque indicating rooms 230-249 were to the right. The doors to the rooms were set back from wrought iron railings that you could look over and spy on the guests in the lobby. Pink plastic flowers in oblong cream boxes were hanging off the railings every four or five feet. Someone in the 1970s must have thought this was a fetching touch.

I finally arrived at room 237 and was looking forward to plopping down on the bed and taking a little snooze. Five a.m. was way too early for this girl to arise from her bed, and I was feeling groggy despite the two thermoses of coffee I'd downed.

Opening the door with the huge key and shouldering in, I pocketed the key, flipped on the light switch on my right. I grunted past the bathroom, and upon entering the room, I yelped. There on the carpet at the foot of the beds was a chalked outline of what was at one time, I assumed, a dead body. And just to add to the mise-en-scène, a brownish stain that must have oozed out of said body formed the shape of the Hispaniola. I backed out of the room much quicker than I had entered and stood with my back against the railing trying to catch my breath. Was this some kind of promotion for a video thriller, or was this the real McCoy?

I gingerly went back into room 237, picked up the phone, and called the front desk.

"Hi, this is Annie Fillmore in two thirty-seven. Is there supposed to be a chalked outline of a dead body in my room?"

"Oh, my God," came the answer.

I darted out of the room and stood at the top of the stairs.

I might as well have shot a gun over the railing, because in what seemed like a minute, there were several people running up the stairs toward me. Dun Wonderly was leading the charge, with Bucky right behind. A third man and a young woman followed Bucky.

"Wail, see, you weren't supposed to be in this room, you were assigned to room two thirty-nine. A little mistake. Heh heh heh. Kind of a little joke, ya see?" Dun expounded.

"No, I don't really see. There must have been a dead body in that room on the blood-soaked carpet," I pronounced. "There was a dead person, right?"

"Hail no. We're an upstanding hotel. Now, for your inconvenience we're going to give you your room free for the duration of your stay. How's that?" he said, looking mighty proud of his generosity. "Now let's all get back to the festivities. And I'd be as happy as a dead pig in the sunshine if you'd keep this to yourself, lit . . . ." He stopped mid-sentence. I swear he was going to call me little lady.

"No problem. Thanks for the free stay, I appreciate it."

I instinctively thought, better go along with this until you find out what's going on.

The third man, who I didn't know, stepped into the room to retrieve my suitcase. "May we bring your luggage to your new room?" he asked.

"No, thanks, I've got it. Just one small case." Unless it was up more stairs, I reflected.

He then handed me the key to room 239.

Bucky stuck out his hand and shook mine, winking at me again, "Hi, I'm Bucky Henderson, nice to meet you. I'm Dun's right-hand man, so if you need anything else, please let me know. I'll take care of it," he said.

I'd just met the guy fifteen minutes ago. He must have met a lot of people since then or had a serious memory problem.

"Christ, Bucky, ya just met her downstairs. Come on," instructed Dun, but I heard him say under his breath, "Bucky, you got shit for brains."

The four of them looked relieved as if they were *live* pigs in the sunshine as they walked toward the staircase. How happy could a dead pig be, anyway? Even in the sunshine? Anyway, I started toward room 239, but stopped short of the door and eyed them as they made their way down the stairs.

"What the *hail* is a matter with you?" Dun barked at the young woman. "What's your name again?"

"Jessica."

"You're farred. Didn't you go ta the meeting 'bout that room? *Nobody* was to be given that room. *Nobody*. I sure as *hail* hope you haven't started a bahn fire. That won't be pretty for you, missy."

The three men stomped down the stairs, leaving Jessica in their wake now sitting on the step she had been standing on, with her head in her hands crying. Geez that seemed harsh. After all, she'd only given me a wrong room key.

Something was rotten in Wonderly. Who did that dead body belong to?

I sighed, reached into my pocket for the new key and realized I still had both keys, room 237 and room 239.

CHAPTER 3

Room 239 was exactly the same as 237 barring the chalked outline of a dead man. Or woman. It could be the taped outline of a dead woman. Couldn't it?

Opening the curtains didn't afford much light, as the room looked out on the back of another building that might have been the bourbon distillery Daisy mentioned. But there was enough light to see that the bedspreads could have been on those beds since the hotel first opened. A sickly sweet smell had been in my nostrils since I'd hit town. That syrupy smell mixed with the lingering cigarette miasma from twenty years of committed smokers was making me bilious. Three days of this?

Assessing the unpalatable options that lay before me, I decided the bed closest to the bathroom was the one for me. With two fingers I gingerly removed the burgundy and pink flowered bedspread and tossed it into the corner of the room. I've read way too many horror stories about what a black light reveals about those things. I tried not to think of who had lain on that thin pale yellow blanket and what they might have left on it. I sure hoped the sheets had been disinfected. Pushing the stiff button on the window air-conditioner, I waited for the first blast of cold air to cut through the funk that suffused the room. Hmm, I thought, when I noticed two doors on either side of the room no doubt connecting me to 237 on one side and room 241 on the other. Not to brag, but that kind of deduction helped me solve a few murders in my recent past.

My head hit the surprisingly fresh-smelling pillow, and I must have drifted off for several hours because when the phone rang I had no idea how much time had passed. I didn't spring to my feet, more rolled over and picked it up.

"Hello?" Who knew I was here?

"Hey, Annie, it's Rob. The Meet and Greet has started. Hope you're gonna join us."

"Oh yeah. Sorry. I fell asleep. Where is it? What do I wear?"

"It's in the Leapin' Lizards Lounge, but I'll meet you at the bottom of the stairs in about fifteen minutes. Come as you are. It's probably way better than what everybody else is wearing," he chuckled.

I freshened up in the bathroom, quickly unpacked my suitcase, and hung up the few things I'd brought. It would have been good if I'd had time to iron my go-to black rayon dress, but I didn't, so a wrinkled dress it was. I tossed some chunky red beads around my neck, pulled on my black leather knee-high boots, and was ready. It wasn't knee-high boot weather in Kentucky that October, but where I come from that's what you wear when the leaves start to turn. They say "When in Rome," but this wasn't Rome. Not even close.

Rob greeted me at the bottom of the steps in a pair of jeans and one of his many short-sleeved plaid shirts. He loved plaid like I loved black.

"See? I knew you'd be better dressed than most of the guests," he said, ever so graciously.

"A bit wrinkled, but that happens when you almost walk in on a dead body in your room."

"Say what?" He stopped and looked at me with something between a frown and a smile. "Are you kidding?" It was a what-are you-talking-about look.

"Haven't you heard? The first room I was assigned had the chalked outline of a dead body. Dun asked me not to say anything to anybody, but I don't suppose he meant you."

"What the hell is that all about," he said, looking truly perplexed.

"Don't tell anybody I told you. I might end up being surrounded by police chalk myself."

"Nah, don't worry. It's probably a prank of some kind, and you got the wrong room. That must be it," he said, but still had a look; was it puzzlement or apprehension?

I knew darn well it wasn't a prank, but I didn't share that news with Rob, and I didn't mention the dried pool of blood. How did I know what he knew? You know?

We walked in silence until we arrived at Leapin' Lizards Lounge, which was filled to the walls with happy video store owners convening and commiserating. He was right. I needn't have worried about my duds. Somebody stuck something on my back, and I almost broke my neck trying to find out what it was.

Rob laughed. "You're not supposed to see it. It's a break-the-ice thing. You have a name on your back, and you have to ask other people questions about who it might be. Like you might say, 'Am I a man or a woman?'" See, that kind of thing."

"What if I don't care whose name is on my back?"

"Come on, it'll be fun. I'll get you a drink. What do you want?"

"Dewar's on the rocks. Thanks."

"Wine or beer," he clarified.

25

"Wine, please. Red."

As Rob made his way over to the bar area, a guy I'd met at a VSDA (Video Store Dealers Association) meeting of the Southern Ohio/Northern Kentucky chapter approached me. Max Helman. Everybody called him Mayo for obvious reasons. He was president of the chapter and called me every two weeks or so to ask me to be on the board. I'd considered it, but I wasn't sure what the VSDA actually did. I thought they just supported stores with X-rated videos that were being harassed by some persnickety members of the public who didn't care for pornography for themselves or anybody else. Hey, porn isn't my preferred film genre, but if those with that kind of sleazy taste like it, so be it.

"Am I a man or a woman?" he asked.

"Gosh, Mayo, if you don't know, how am I supposed to?"

"No, not me, the name on my back. I'm all man, you can be sure of that," he said straightening his robust stature to what was probably a full 5'11". His eyes were dark blue, and one of them was lazy and seemed to look off in a different direction from me, and his moustache kind of twitched over his big smile.

"Oh. Turn around and let me see who you are."

Dolly Parton, read the tag on his back.

"You're all woman," I said, laughing.

"Dolly Parton," he guessed correctly.

"Wow."

"Not that hard. This is a country music kind of group. Who's the most womanly country singer you can think of? Dolly Parton."

I couldn't quarrel with him, and I didn't want to. I was still feeling fritzy from the thought that I had almost shared a room with a corpse, and

I didn't feel too sociable. What's more, if the name of a country singer was taped on my back, I'd be lost, unless I was Patsy Cline.

Turning around, I began walking toward the exit.

"Where you going?" Mayo asked with surprise.

"I need some air. I'll be back. I just have to catch a breeze before I really get into this game."

"Ok. I'll be here when you get back," he said.

I had no intention of returning. I was in search of room spray to freshen up 239, and, if I was lucky, maybe find a nice restaurant where I could dine solo. All this hubbub was not agreeing with me.

The girl at the front desk told me there was a pharmacy and a restaurant on Pleasant Street, which ran directly in front of the hotel. "Just take a right when you get out of the parking lot."

I walked out of the lobby doors and stopped to look around. It looked like someone had paved over the Sahara Desert. The parking lot was not even half full. Who were they expecting? That damn lot went on forever. But then I remembered hearing they also had concerts in the Wonderly Arena attached to the hotel. So maybe they needed all that concrete. Not that night though.

CHAPTER 4

The ten-minute walk to downtown Wonderly was dark and sticky. Fall had definitely not arrived in this part of Kentucky. I passed a copse of trees on my right before coming to a huge construction site. If a sign indicated what it was going to be, I missed it. Walmart? Apartments? A better hotel? The opposite side of the street was peppered with apartments and office buildings. Ahead I spotted light and what looked like an actual little village.

The brick sidewalk was lit by gaslight-style street lamps. Cars crawled by slowly in both directions. The hotel might have looked like a prison, but the town seemed quaint, with actual shops people frequented. By the time I passed a florist, Boo-Kay (seriously), my boots were pinching and my toes were sweating.

Next to Boo-Kay was a pharmacy looking like most pharmacies do—like they're not going to have room spray. I was just happy they were still open at seven thirty.

"Good evening, miss. How may I help you?" called an actual pharmacist from the back.

"Hi. I'm looking for room freshener. Do you happen to have anything that would pass for that?"

"Pass for that? I'm not catchin' you, ma'am," he said, coming out from behind his counter toward me.

"Do you have anything I might *use* as a room freshener?" I explained more slowly as if he were hard of hearing. But I suddenly realized, it wasn't him, it was me. I was the out-of-towner who didn't speak in the native tongue. I might as well have been yodeling.

"Oh yes. Do you have any?"

"We have this Glade Country Pottery Air-Freshener that's on special. It's been mighty popular with the ladies. Has a real nice aroma," he replied, using his best sales pitch.

"You've saved my life, or at least my breath. I'm staying at The Dunbar Hotel, and my room smells of cigarettes," I said.

"I betcha all those rooms smell of cigarettes. This is Kentucky, ma'am. But this should do the trick," he said, ringing up my first Kentucky purchase of six dollars and ninety-nine cents.

"Thank you kindly," I said as I opened the door to leave. Thank you kindly? I hadn't even been here one day, and I already sounded like Scarlett O'Hara.

Continuing on down Pleasant Street, the rest of the stores were closed. I passed an antique store, a hardware store, Delilah's Candies, and, happily, came upon The Wonder, a restaurant that looked quite nice and was open. I didn't pass that one. I entered. I guess Daisy was right; Dun Wonderly did own almost everything in this town.

So, two nice surprises: air freshener and a pleasant restaurant on Pleasant Street to offset the earlier unpleasantness.

A young man greeted me from behind his maître d' stand. "Welcome to The Wonder," he said. "Do you have a reservation?"

"Gosh, no. Do I need one?"

"Will someone be joining you this evening?"

"No. Just me."

"We'll be delighted to serve you," he said, grabbing a menu. "Please follow me."

I always wish they'd say, "Please walk this way," so I could imitate their walk. But they never do.

The lovely large square room was dimly lit by small lamps on every table. Against the left wall were booths to seat four people, six if you squished. Tables of varying sizes filled the center of the room. One large group of people wearing paper party hats were seated toward the back, yukking it up and celebrating.

Jeff, as his name tag read, seated me at a table for two outside a bar area that looked like an extra room, but the wide arched opening allowed me to see what was happening in there. It's always good to see what the bar people are up to.

"Brian will be taking care of you this evening, but if you need anything further, please let me know." I didn't even flinch when he removed the cutlery for another diner at my table. As he walked away, I noticed his ironed khaki pants and blue oxford-cloth shirt made the perfect ensemble for this place.

A few minutes passed before Brian came over to introduce himself and to hand me an impressive wine list. He was much more casual in demeanor than Jeff. He wore khakis, too, but with a white shirt, sleeves rolled up.

"No wine right now, Brian. I'll have a Dewar's on the rocks with a twist please."

"Great night for a Dewar's," he concurred.

Ahh. Things were looking up.

Glancing around the room, I saw a smattering of people settled comfortably in the green leather booths or, like me, at a table with green chairs.

The little lamp on the white tablecloth made me feel at home. Well, a much better appointed home, but home.

Blown-up black-and-white photographs of horses hung on the wall. Floodlights not only lit the horses but made a nice arc on the brick wall.

Brian came over and asked if I was ready to order.

"In a moment, Brian. This place is charming. Does Dun Wonderly own it?" I asked.

"No. Andy owns it. He's Dun's brother," Brian offered. "He also owns the horse farm about a mile down the road from the hotel, Wonder Farm."

"Does he go by the name Wonder?" I inquired.

"No. He goes by Andy Wonderly, but he told me he wanted to make sure people didn't think Dun owned his farm, so he left off the 'ly'."

"Makes sense," I said, although what kind of sense did that make? Dun still could have owned it. Maybe he should have called it "Definitely Not Dun Wonderly's Farm."

"What do you recommend?" Why do I bother asking when I never take their suggestion? I skimmed the menu until I spotted Shrimp and Grits with Andouille sausage. I looked up as Brian was saying something about seared something wrapped in something. It might have been intriguing, but I had mentally already eaten half the shrimp and grits.

Just as I was about to give my order, a kerfuffle was taking place in the bar area. Jessica, the young woman from the hotel who had just been fired, was trying to get up on a bar stool, but kept missing. The stool was high, she was short, and it seemed like she might have stopped at another bar already. A young man entered the scene and gallantly helped her reach the height she needed to get her fanny on that green leather bar stool.

I ordered, happy to have a full view of what was going on in the bar. If you know me at all you know this: when I'm in a crowd I consider other people's business my own. And I don't miss much. The mystery of room 237 was still percolating in the back of my mind. What was the real story? I was determined to find out something before the evening was over.

Jessica and her Sir Galahad were by now yelling at each other. He left in what looked like a huff, and Jessica started crying—again. Not a great day for this girl.

My dinner had not yet been served, so I took the opportunity to go to the bar.

"Jessica? Hi. I'm Annie Fillmore, the woman who I'm afraid might have started all this," I said.

"I remember you," she whimpered with mucous coming out of her perfect nose onto her perfect top lip.

"I'm so sorry. I know this isn't your fault. Is there anything I can do to help?" I asked, putting my arm around her shoulder on her washed-out jean jacket. She was more beautiful close-up. Her eyes matched her jacket, but were blurry with tears, and her huge amount of curly blond hair framed her sweet face with those lips. I could have kissed those lips if I'd been of another persuasion.

"It's not your fault," she hiccupped. "We can never do anything right by Dun. But that *was* a big eff-up on my part. We did have a meeting about that room. I don't know what I was thinking. It was just so darn busy today, I didn't know whether to scratch my watch or wind my butt."

These are colorful people in these here parts!

"What happened in that room that it's off-limits?" I asked boldly.

"Are you kiddin' me? I can't tell you that. That's what the meeting was about. We're not even suppose' to know what happened in there even though we kinda know," she said, her eyes clearing a bit. This kid needed food and a cup of coffee.

"I'm just about to have dinner," I said. "Will you join me?"

"Okay, and also I need another brewski to calm my nerves."

"Food and a brewski it is," I replied, helping her off the stool and over to my table where my food was waiting.

We ordered a burger and a Bud Light for Jessica. I was still working on my Scotch and sizing her up to decide my best approach. How could I worm some information out of her about what she and everybody else knew that I didn't?

"Will you be able to find another job here?" I asked.

"Probably not. Dun owns everything in town where I'd want to work. I'll go to Lou'ville or Lexington. I'll find something. But working at Wonderly was good, even if he's a jerk. You get to meet the studio reps, and they are very generous with their handouts—if Dun doesn't get to them first."

"What do you mean? Get to the reps first?"

"No, get the goodies they hand out. Last Christmas one of the studios gave the inside reps a fifty-dollar gift certificate to Venus de Milo. You know, the lingerie place. But Dun found out about it and took all the certificates and kept them for himself."

"How many reps are there?"

"Twenty inside reps right now."

"What on earth would he do with twenty gift certificates for ladies lingerie?" I asked, dumbfounded.

"Who knows? Word is he's getting divorced from Sugar and has a young girlfriend, but even she can't use all that stuff. She only has two tits," she said swigging the beer Brian had brought her. "Whatever he did with them you can bet he made money, or chased another girl."

"Did this have anything to do with the dead body in room two thirty-seven?"

"You trying to trick me?" She squinted at me.

"Just wondering if there was a connection, that's all. Look Jessica, I don't live in Wonderly, and the only people I know down here are Rob Woodbury and my inside rep, Linda. I'm just curious since I did see that chalked outline of a body; and I think it would be good for someone else to know what happened besides you and your co-workers. You know? Just to be safe." I was definitely scheming to get the real dope. Would Miss Marple play it any differently? Kinsey Milhone?

In answer she raised her hand for Brian to bring her another beer. "The guy who was killed in room two thirty-seven was Bobby Crane, the sales manager of Dun's company, Bare Bottom Babes."

"What is Bare Bottom Babes?" I asked, narrowing my eyes in prejudgment.

"You know those wet T-shirt videos that are so popular? Well, Dun thought those videos were keener than frog's hair so he wanted to get in on it. Don't you carry the T-shirt videos in your store? We can't keep 'em in stock; and Dun's banking the same for his BBB videos." My Scotch was now mostly pale water, but that was okay with me, because Jessica was singing like a drunken bird.

"What did the police say about Bobby Crane? Did they question everybody?" I prodded.

"Never heard a word about it. Nobody saw them carry a body out. Never saw anything on the news. It's like he never existed," she declared.

"Surely he must have a family who wondered what happened to him. Somebody?"

"You'd think. The only thing I know is that Rachel checked Bobby in on October ninth, gave him the key to room two thirty-seven, and we never saw him again. The next day Rachel said Bobby's room registration was erased from the computer. Then we had that meeting about room two thirty-seven having some safety issues. We were not to put anybody in that room. But I did. I put you in there."

"How did you know he was murdered and didn't just leave?"

"Rosa, one of the housekeepers, saw him the next day. She went into the room to clean, and she saw the body. She doesn't speak English that well, and she was spooked, that's for sure. We told her to be quiet. She understood that.

"Bottom line is Bobby was a bad-ass, and tried anything and everything to get laid–tried it with me with some cock-and-bull story. At least I think it was cock-and-bull. If it wasn't, whew."

"What was the cock-and-bull story?"

"What? I'm not telling you. It's probably not even true. You can't always believe Bobby. Or couldn't," she slurred.

"How do you know about the wet T-shirt videos? Do you work as a sales rep *and* at the front desk?" I wondered out loud.

"When one of the girls in the back is out, one of us from the front will cover if it's busy. Even though we don't know the stock as well as the regulars, we can take orders, and that's what Dun likes," she said shrugging her shoulders.

"So about these BBB videos, how long have they been available?" I prodded.

"We all knew he was making them. He had a photographer from Lou'ville come up and do some demos in one of those back rooms he fitted out with beach scenes. He was paying good money for any girl who wanted to bare her bottom. No faces, he promised, so a lot of girls thought that was an easy way to make some extra cash. He also promised no names would be made public. The videos were taken at night so nobody except the girls showing their asses knew who was involved. We all thought there might be more going on in those back rooms than photography, if you know what I mean."

"You mean sex?" You can't put one over on Sherlock Holmes. "Do you think he paid more if they had sex with him?"

"Oh yeah. Lots of money."

"Those videos never did see the light of day or into the customers' stores, because he said they just weren't real looking. That's when he took the girls down to the Bahamas, so he could get real live footage on a real live beach."

"Could he do that on a beach in full view of everybody? That doesn't sound right."

"One of the girls told me he rented his own beachfront, and he put those high flimsy fences around so nobody could see what was going on. After they finally were finished, he had a big viewing, and honestly, even though it was kind of icky seeing those butts and guessing which belonged to who, it was pretty great. That beach looked beautiful."

Oh my!

"May I interest you in dessert, ladies," asked Brian hopefully.

Jessica shook her head no.

"Thanks, Brian, not for me either. I'll just take the check."

"I'm watching my waistline," Jessica explained. "I'm getting myself to Hollywood for real and gonna try to become famous. That's why I didn't show my butt just to make some cash. What's a couple a thousand dollars compared to the millions I'm gonna make?" she said proudly, like she'd already banked those notes.

Stranger things have happened. She was a beauty. Maybe Hollywood needed another blonde.

"Can you give me your phone number in case something happens, or I need to get in touch with you," I asked, handing her the little notebook I always keep handy for just such an eventuality.

She scribbled her number down and handed it to me. "But I'm not telling you anything more. I probably shouldn't even have told you this."

"There's more?" I probed.

"You have no idea," she said, getting up from the table.

"How are you getting home? I don't think it's a good idea for you to drive," I said in my best maternal voice.

"No, ma'am. It's fine. I walked here. I can walk home. It's not that far."

We hugged like two old friends, and off we went in different directions.

CHAPTER 5

The Meet and Greet party was breaking up by the time I got back to the hotel. Thankfully, nobody I knew saw me, so I didn't have to lie. Not that I wouldn't lie, it's just better not to as my Moms repeatedly tell me. "There's no need not to tell the truth. You'll feel better, dear," Helen would say. To be honest, it never made me feel bad to prevaricate a little.

All I could think of while climbing those stairs was laying my head on that clean-smelling pillowcase right after I eliminated the cigarette smell from the room with my Glade purchase.

Directly after turning on the light I sat down on the edge of the bed without the slimy cover and pulled off my boots. I collapsed back on the bed and savored my shoeless feet. Walking on the carpet that no doubt had been tread upon by hundreds of pairs of grungy feet made me shiver; but fatigue won, and I grabbed the Glade from my bag to freshen up the place. The directions read:

- Remove the tube, cap, and pottery vessel from the box.

- Pointing the fragrance tube away from your face, firmly pinch the narrow portion of the tube and snip the end.

- Gently squeeze the entire contents of the fragrance tube into the pottery.

- Snap the plastic cap into place so that it is flush with the vessel.

- Within several hours the fragrance will absorb into the pottery. Blah blah blah.

Several hours? I could be asphyxiated by that time. Plus I didn't have scissors to snip off the narrow portion of the tube. Rummaging through my bag I realized the only semi-sharp thing I had were tweezers. I operated on the slim tube with the head of the tweezers and made only a slight dent.

I fumbled in the closet for my sneakers, put them on, and headed for the front desk for a proper pair of scissors. Halfway down the stairs I thought I saw somebody walk under them coming from the lobby. Whoever it was had big curly blond hair and a blue denim jacket; but by the time I got to the bottom they were gone. It was ten forty-five, and the rest of the lobby was empty.

"Was that Jessica I just saw coming through the lobby?" I asked the girl at the front desk.

"Jessica who?" she responded with a slight chill to her voice.

I noticed her name tag said RACHEL. Was this the same Rachel that Jessica had mentioned earlier?

"Jessica who got fired today?"

"No. She was fired. She wouldn't be here."

"May I have a seven a.m. wake-up call?" I requested.

"Room number?"

"I'm in room two thirty-nine. And do you have a pair of scissors I can borrow?"

"Scissors?"

Isn't that what they're called in Kentucky?

"Yes. Scissors."

"Let me take a look around."

She returned in under a minute with a huge pair of scissors. I would have made a joke, but Rachel didn't seem to have a sense of humor. She could have been a second Robin Williams for all I knew. She was hiding it well.

Upon returning to my room I found a piece of paper under my door:

SATURDAY ～ OCTOBER 19

8 a.m. –Breakfast, Meeting Room 2, sponsored by Universal Studios – *Backdraft*

10 a.m. – 5 p.m. – Convention Floor Open

10 a.m. – 5 p.m. – Warehouse Open for Purchases

Noon – Lunch – Meeting Room 1, sponsored by Touchstone – *What About Bob?*

4:00 – 5:00 p.m. – Marketing Magic with Mark Heyward – Meeting Room 2

6:00 – 7:00 p.m. – Cocktails in Leapin' Lizards Lounge, sponsored by Columbia – *City Slickers*

7:30 p.m. – Dinner, Dining Room 1, sponsored by Disney – *Fantasia*

9:30 p.m. – The Bluegrass Fellas, Wonderly Arena – Wonderly Entertainment

Heeding it almost no attention except breakfast at eight, I hurried to my Glade.

I snipped off the end of the tube, dumped it into the pottery base, secured the top, and waited for the powdery smell to diffuse the hell out of that room.

Face washed, teeth brushed, nightgown on I decided to call the store to see if it was still there and how the day had gone without me.

Me: Hi, Josh, it's Annie, how'd the day go? Good news, bad news?

Josh: Hey, Annie. How you doing down there?

Me: Tired at the moment. How'd the day go?

Josh: Good. It rained like crazy, and the store was packed. Great night, actually.

Me: Bad news?

Josh: None, unless you count that we never stopped from seven on.

Me: Well, that's good news, too. Thanks so much Josh for all the work. Neil with you to help out?

Josh: Yeah. He just left. He said he was getting an early start tomorrow.

Me: Okay. Thanks again. Get some rest.

As for me, I was so exhausted, narcolepsy sounded like a bit of a treat.

CHAPTER 6

At seven a.m. my wake-up call interrupted a dream about puppies (always a good sign, Helen told me).

After a hot shower, I had the usual battle with my hair. It wants to have its way; I want to have mine. Sadly, it usually turns out somewhere in the middle, which would find neither my hair nor me on the cover of any magazines except, possibly, *MAD*. So be it. I donned my jeans and a white shirt, new blue sweater, and yellow Chuck Taylors. At least my feet were happy.

Peering over the wrought-iron railing I could see the lobby abuzz with conventioneers ready for the big day. I hadn't seen any celebrities yet, but then I hadn't partaken in much of the happenings. It was hard not to miss Daisy in her bright yellow pants and orange-and-yellow flowered blouse as she chatted cheerfully with Mayo. Hermy, ever the obedient spouse, was standing quietly by her side. She must have had me on radar because she looked up to where I was standing, waved, and beckoned to me to come down. Which I did. Hermy and I were both the obedient types, it seemed.

"Where's your bag? You need something to put the goodies in," she reminded me.

"Won't they have bags?"

"Not big ones," she said shaking her head, perplexed with my lack of acquisitiveness no doubt.

Daisy and I followed the crowd through a door at the back of the lobby leading to the meeting rooms. We found room 2, which was large and set up with round tables for eight, the walls decorated with *Backdraft* posters. Each table featured a centerpiece made of an upside-down fireman's hat filled with red and orange carnations and some greens to set them off. On each chair was a large Universal Studio tote bag full of the proverbial goodies. I set the tote bag on the floor next to my chair and sat down while some others were oohing and ahhing over the contents of said bag. They *were* nice: *Backdraft* T-shirt, cap, posters, stickers, and a koozie to keep your beer cold while fighting a fire.

Daisy, Hermy, Mayo, and Rob were already seated at a table. A couple who had a store somewhere in Indiana were also there along with Tina, an inside rep. I noticed one gorgeous young woman seated at each of the other tables. All inside reps, I gathered. What was in the water down here? They could have been movie stars themselves. I was pleased our table was toward the back so I had a good view of the others. It's always good to know who you're breakfasting with. Scanning the room, I tried to guess which one of those beauties was my inside rep, Linda. We had become fast friends over the phone, and I wondered if our phone chemistry would translate face-to-face.

Once everyone was seated, Dun Wonderly appeared at the front of the room and introduced Matt Melson, a Universal rep.

"Here he is folks," Dun said with his arm slung around Matt's shoulder. "Santy Claus with goodies for all you good little video store owners. Heh heh heh. Ya better hold onto those bags, or I might just take 'em mahself. Heh heh heh."

Was this guy serious? I looked at the other faces around the table to see if anybody else was rolling their eyes, but I seemed to be rolling solo.

Matt took the microphone from Dun. "Thanks, Dun. Let's give a big thank you to Dunbar for putting this wonderful convention together."

We all clapped, with a few woot woots from the peanut gallery.

"Thank you all for coming. We hope you enjoy your breakfast. But before we start serving, we'd like to give you a preview of *Backdraft,* which promises to be a big renter. When you've got star power like Kurt Russell and Billy Baldwin fighting fires in Chicago, with love stories and crime to add heat, you have a sure winner. This thriller also stars Robert De Niro and Donald Sutherland, so this one is going to be renting like, well, wildfire. And now. . . . *Backdraft.*

The lights lowered, and a big screen in the front of the room came to life with the slow spinning globe against a blue sky behind the Universal logo. It never fails to give me a chill of excitement when a movie starts, even a trailer. I was happy to be in the video business whether it paid or not.

Rushing fire that looked like waves of lava and sirens in the background set the scene for what was to come. And then the scream. It was so close it seemed to come from behind us not from the screen. Nobody did anything until the second scream. Rob got up so fast that his chair fell behind him as he bounded out of the room. The trailer played on. Then the dazzling reps got up and scurried out of the room. Then more commotion. Finally the overhead lights snapped on and the trailer stopped.

"What's going on?" I asked nobody in particular.

We just sat there dumbly as servers started arriving from the back with trays of breakfast. If I didn't get a cup of coffee soon I was going to be screaming just like the headache that was crawling over my forehead. Later I wished that the headache was just from not having my first cup of coffee.

I excused myself and went out to the lobby, where some of the girls were holding each other and crying. Rob came toward me, "Go back inside,

Annie. There's been a terrible accident. You don't need to be involved in this."

"What kind of an accident? Was somebody hurt?"

"It's a warehouse accident. Something happened, and one of the shelves fell and crushed someone. She's dead."

I knew it was Jessica without even asking. I started to get the shakes, and Rob looked at me weirdly. "You okay?"

"It's Jessica isn't it?" I blubbered.

"What the… how would you know that? How do you know her?"

That first whiff of death surrounded me like a shroud.

"We have to go someplace and talk. Someplace where nobody can see or hear us."

"You go back inside and have breakfast." He checked his watch, "I'll meet you at nine fifteen in the parking lot. I have a red pickup with Indiana plates."

As I sat back down in my seat, Dun Wonderly was in front again about to address the group. "I'm just as sad as hell to have to tell you folks we've had a terrible accident in the warehouse. One of the girls was *prolly* doin' what she shouldn'ta been doin', climbin' up the shelf to get a video, and bam it fell over on her and kilt her dead. Sad as hell. Jessica was a good girl. Just doin' the wrong thing."

A large police officer standing next to Dun was shifting his weight from foot to foot. The impressive silver badge on his chest said Chief.

A man at one of the front tables raised his hand. "Yes, Lester," Mr. Wonderly said. "Lester's one of Wonderly's video store owners: Video and Bait, right Lester?" Wonderly asked.

"Right, Dun. But where's Chief Danvers? Where's Cal?" Lester asked. "I han't seen him 'round for week or so."

"Yeah, kinda sudden, guess you'd say. Cal up and retired a month early. Ya know he loves his place on the Land 'tween the Lakes, and that's where he's off ta," Wonderly said.

"That's weird though. Didn't say good-bye t'all." Lester whined, scratching his head.

"Ya need to ask Bucky 'bout it. He knows the details. They're related in some way t'other. Now on to business," said Dun, cutting off the conversation. "Let me introduce you to our *new* chief of police, Chief Denny Earl."

"Hi folks. This is a heck of a welcome to our fair town, but, sadly, that's life. The death may be an accident as Dun says, or it might not be. For that reason we're asking you not to leave Wonderly tomorrow as you may have planned on doing. If this thing is something other than an accident, well, everybody in the hotel has to be questioned."

The room started humming.

Daisy raised her hand.

"Yes miss?" Chief Earl nodded in her direction.

"Will the convention floor be opened? And can we still go to the warehouse to purchase the sale videos?"

"The convention floor will be opened as scheduled. You may leave the hotel but not the town. We'll clear the scene in the warehouse by 'bout three o'clock. You can check back then to see if it's open. So, to be clear, no trips to Lexington or Lou'ville." That's how they pronounce Louisville...Lou'ville.

My breakfast of scrambled eggs, bacon, and a pancake was stone cold. Thankfully, there was a carafe of coffee that was hot. And the side of fruit was edible. I poured that black magic into the hefty white cup and sighed.

"We don't mind staying a couple of more days. Do you?" asked Daisy.

"I sure hadn't planned on it. I have a small crew, so I just hope they can handle the extra hours. So, yes, I mind staying. But I guess I can't go against police orders."

No! I couldn't stay a few more days. Not even one more day. My store might be nothing more than a heap of rubble if I didn't get back to oversee what was going on. Chief Earl looked able enough, but I've known police and detectives who looked capable but acted like the Keystone Kops in action. Maybe I needed to snoop around to accelerate the proceedings.

My watch said eight forty, and I needed to call Neil or Marilyn to see if they could figure out who could work and when. My worst fear, a closed store, took hold. I looked for my bag of *Backdraft* swag, but it wasn't on the floor where I'd left it.

"Daisy, did you see what happened to my *Backdraft* tote?"

"Oh, you left, so I figured you didn't want it." She pulled up a large laundry bag from under the table that was full to the brim with totes and all the goodies in them. "Here, take one of mine," she offered.

She was the opposite of Dun's Santy Claus. Good grief, she was as wily as the Grinch under a Whoville Christmas tree.

"Thank you kindly," I said. This time I meant to be snarky, and I channeled Scarlett O'Hara with a raised eyebrow for good measure.

I walked swiftly to the lobby and up the stairs to my room. Eight forty-five … Marilyn would be in the midst of her regular infernal morning, so I decided to wake Neil. He wouldn't be up, but he'd like the drama of a death as much as he'd like more sleep.

"Hey, sorry to wake you, but I have a problem," I reported to Neil.

"What kind of a problem?" he asked drowsily.

I told him.

"Don't worry about it, we'll figure it out and have it covered. I prom-ise. But call me and let me know what's happening. Do you want me to come down?"

"No. I want you to stay there and keep the store afloat until I get back."

"Yes, ma'am," he answered sarcastically.

A drizzly, grey day greeted me as I exited the front doors of the hotel in search of Rob's red pickup truck. I saw flashing headlights three rows back signaling where Rob was. As I dashed through lines of parked cars to his truck, I saw that Rob had opened the passenger door for me.

"Why is this truck so high?" I grunted.

"It's a truck, not your low-to-the-ground Honda."

"Huh." Had I never been in a pickup before?

"I'll drive down to the lake and you can tell me what's going on, or what you think is going on."

I gave him a sideways glare. Rob is the type who, unlike me, minds his own business. He actually frowns on knowing personal things about people. We're so different. All I knew was what Jessica told me. What I *didn't* know was the truth of what Bobby Crane told Jessica. Her untimely death suggested that she might have found out it was true, and someone didn't like it one little bit.

We drove silently down Pleasant Street past the stores I had walked by the night before and more stores beyond those. I then noticed stores on the left-hand side of the street, mostly antique stores and antique malls. After that a Baptist church, gas station, and a parking lot. We continued on Pleasant Street until a bumpy road veered off to the left. Wonderly Acres Mobile Home Park was on the right as we made our way to the lake. A stone wall with a fancy sign at the entrance made it look welcoming.

At the end of the road, Rob pulled into a dirt parking lot set back from the lake.

"Is this lake called Wonderly, too?" I asked.

"No. It's Lake Pleasant. That's where the street name comes from, I'm guessing. Lake Pleasant. Pleasant Street. Nice fishing, crappies mostly. After a rough meeting I'll come down here to get my mind off it and sit with the fish."

"Better than sleeping with the fish," I wisecracked.

He turned to look at me. "So what do you think is going on that you need to tell me?"

"Well, first of all, Jessica is the girl who Dun Wonderly fired yesterday after she mistakenly put me in the wrong room, where somebody was found dead last week. Remember I told you this last night, Rob? Anyway this morning when he was telling us that Jessica was dead, he never mentioned that she was no longer with Wonderly."

"He's just being careful. He probably didn't want to say he'd fired her," Rob riposted.

"What was she doing there if she'd been fired? When I came down to get scissors from the front desk last night about ten forty-five, I could swear Jessica was running toward the back. What's back there?"

"The offices and the warehouse."

"The girl at the front desk, Rachel, must have seen her, because Jessica was coming from the lobby. But Rachel said she wasn't there. That was odd."

"Rachel and I are buddies. I'll see if I can find out what she knows, but she must be pretty bummed, and she might want to cover it up if it was Jessica, if she thought Jess would get into trouble. But I'll try," he said with finality.

"Trouble? She's dead. That's about as much trouble as you can get into don't you think?"

He didn't respond.

I didn't want to divulge everything Jessica told me, because I had no idea if Rob was even peripherally involved. My first thought was, I doubt it. But as I've already mentioned, my first thoughts have often gotten me into a world of trouble. Also, sharing the kind of information I had might compromise his job. He had a wife and family who were no doubt more important to him than my incompetent sleuthing, no matter where it led.

Backing up the red truck, Rob said, "I don't know what's going on or what you think is going on, but you better be careful if you know stuff you're not supposed to know. Dun Wonderly knows a lot of people, some I wouldn't want to meet in a dark alley if you get my point."

Point taken but, actually, I wouldn't even want to meet Dun Wonderly in a dark alley.

"Maybe, but I have to get back to Annie's, and I don't have a lot of confidence that the Wonderly police are going to solve this by Monday. I might have to poke around a bit to help things along. You know the last chief kind of took off in the night to some lake without anybody knowing about it. Not exactly Eliot Ness," I grumbled.

"Eliot Ness was a government agent, not the local police," he corrected me.

"Whatever."

CHAPTER 7

Dead bodies or not it was time for the convention I had come to Wonderly to attend.

Rob scrambled out of the truck, "Hey, I gotta get going. I'm one of the hosts this morning. I'll see you in there."

I crossed the busy lobby and went through the doorway as I had done that morning for breakfast and the night before for Leapin' Lizards Lounge. Past them, the carpeted corridor to the convention floor ahead was hung with movie posters, signed celebrity photos, and photos of Dun and celebrities. There was even a signed photo of Kurt Russell. It was impossible to take time to look at all of them because there were so many people trying to get to the "floor" as they called it. Where did they all come from? The Dunbar couldn't sleep more than 300, 350 at the most. But it was packed with, I guess, video store owners of every stripe–the dumpy to the dolled-up.

A lighted theater marquee with bright blue trim welcomed us:

NOW SHOWING

WONDERLY ENTERTAINMENT

1991

People rushed the entrance like Black Friday at Macy's. For a moment I thought maybe this was going to be more exciting than I'd hoped. But my heart sank when the first thing I saw was a huge, maybe eight foot, cardboard cutout standee of one of the Bare Bottom Babes looking over her shoulder and baring a sumptuous behind. The Babe was nude save a short pink tutu… more like a low belt, but the point was made. Her face peeked out from under a pink cotton sun hat. But there was a bit of face, and I thought Jessica said those girls were anonymous.

The booth that went with that beautiful bottom was decorated with tropical motifs, and the freebies were paper leis in the same pink color as the tutu. Standing behind the booth was one of Wonderly's comely inside reps wearing the same blue WELCOME TO WONDERLY T-shirt that Bucky Henderson was wearing yesterday. As I looked around, I realized everybody who worked for Wonderly was wearing that shirt. There was a pile of business cards on the counter that read BOBBY CRANE, SALES MANAGER, BARE BOTTOM BABES, INC. Somebody wasn't paying attention to detail. If a dead body is detail.

The main reason for my attending the convention was to shop for affordable software for my new computer. We also needed blank VHS tapes and cases for cds and video games. I was also considering some shelving and a few other items. In short, boring stuff. But the music and laughter from what I assumed were the studio booths beckoned me. Doesn't take much.

The lines were long for the three plum spots in the corners of the floor: Columbia's *City Slickers,* Universal's *Backdraft,* and Touchstone's *What About Bob?* The center of the room was reserved for *Fantasia,* and that line was like a great serpent, so I walked the aisles, waiting for something to jump out at me. And it did. As he grabbed my arm, I recognized Red Neck Ricky from one of the wrestling tapes I carried in the store. "Hey, little lady, come on over here and be friendly," he said smiling. When Ricky called me "little lady," he was being literal. He stood about seven feet tall and weighed probably three hundred pounds, with biceps about as big around as my waist. His curly red beard tickled my forehead when he sat me on his lap. "We could be twins with our curly hair," he said, ruffling my ringlets.

By this time a small crowd had gathered. One of his admirers called out, "Hey, Ricky, how you doin'?"

"I'm happier than ol' Blue layin' on the porch, chewin on a big ol' catfish head. How about you?"

"'Bout the same," someone laughingly answered behind me

"Hey thanks, Annie," he said, reading the name off my badge. "You've been a good sport so I'm going to give you something special. He handed me a plastic bag with his photo on the front and something inside.

I walked away and took a T-shirt out of the plastic bag. A friend and I both could have fit in that shirt. I thanked him and moved on to the Playboy booth. Well, I passed the Playboy booth. It was one thing standing next to Ricky looking like a munchkin, and another standing next to a Playboy bunny looking like a puffy munchkin. The bunnies didn't seem as jolly as Ricky anyway.

Rounding the corner I saw Rob in an exit well looming over Rachel, the girl at the front desk the night before. He was also wearing the requisite blue Wonderly T-shirt. She was talking, and he was patting her on the shoulder. He looked like a teacher comforting a student who just received a D on her report card. I sure hoped he was getting some juicy information from her for my murder inquiry. Fierce questions swam in my mind like a shark tank full of squid. Why had Bobby Crane been killed? How was I going to find out how Bobby Crane and Jessica died and if their deaths were related? How soon was I going to get back to Annie's?

It was eleven fifteen by my watch. Lunch was at noon in one of the dining rooms, so I had a little time to go to the *City Slickers* booth. The line had shrunk so I stepped behind a big guy with a white T-shirt that read CHICKEN VIDEO. He turned around and I smiled. "That's the name of your store, Chicken Video?" I asked. "Yes, ma'am. Kind of lucked out on that one. I bought the Chicken 'N Stuff store, so I just taped over the 'N Stuff with Video. Saved me a boatload. This here," he said, pointing to the back of his shirt, "is marketin'."

"Great idea."

Mr. Chicken Video was next in line to enter the attraction, so I waited patiently.

The *City Slickers* booth was dressed up like a scene from an old western movie complete with sagebrush, a floor full of straw, and couple of big tree stumps. They had a life-size, stuffed Norman, the calf Billy Crystal birthed and fell in love with in the movie. While the trailer played on the wall, the Columbia rep, Mark, was promoting the video and taking photos of conventioneers with Norman.

When it was my turn, I knelt down next to Norman, who looked like the work of a taxidermist, but was a plush toy. Hollywood illusion. The light-fingered Daisy Dixon was right, I needed another suitcase to put in all the goodies like the *City Slickers* swag. I still had about twenty minutes until lunch, so I headed to my room to freshen up.

As I was ascending the stairs, I saw Rob over my shoulder with a few other people on their way up in the glass elevator. I hoofed it to the elevator doors on the second floor to wait for him. An older gentleman with a badge that said CAP'N JETH'S VIDEO got off on the second floor. Rob didn't, so I got on.

"Hey, I thought your room was on two," he said.

"What floor are you on?" I asked.

"Three," he answered, and as the doors opened, we both got off. "What's going on?" he inquired.

"I saw you speaking to Rachel and wondered what she said."

"Yeah, we need to talk. Come to my room," he whispered.

He looked around before he put his key in the lock.

"All clear," I announced, having scoped out the surroundings.

He shook his head in what I thought might be annoyance. I ignored it and stepped behind him into his room, laid out exactly the same as rooms 237 and 239. He motioned me into the bathroom, and once inside he turned on the water in the sink and in the shower. "Rumor has it that Dun has bugged all the rooms, so we need to speak softly."

"Seriously? Could he do that? Even in the bathroom?" I said, alarmed.

"The question and answer is would he do it and can he do it? Yes. Maybe not in the bathroom, but just to be safe, the water doesn't hurt.

But it's crazier than even you think. Rachel told me stuff this morning that almost blew my head off. To start, that *was* the outline of Bobby Crane you saw. A dead Bobby Crane. The girls at the front desk had told Dun they heard what sounded like a shot and couldn't get an answer when they knocked on the door. Dun pooh-poohed them. Said everything was great. Not to worry. Just a champagne bottle popping."

"How would Rachel know all of this?" I asked.

"Amber told her. She was outside Dun's office filing her day's cards, and she overheard Dun and Cal talking. Cal received an anonymous call to go to the hotel and look in Room 237. He found Bobby's body and traced the white chalk around it as they always do. Dun had a fit. He said, "There can't be any dead bodies at The Dunbar. Get rid of it. Put it somewhere else. Anywhere. But not here. I want it gone by the end of the night. Heah?"

"How could Dun give the chief of police orders?" I asked.

"When you own the town as Dun does, I guess everybody takes his orders," Rob explained.

"And what happened to that guy, Cal? The chief of police? Somebody was asking Dun today at breakfast what happened to him. Seems he just disappeared."

"How the hell do I know? I feel like I'm in the middle of a B movie," he huffed.

"Oh. And I have a question for you," he continued. "Did Jessica tell you her boyfriend was Ty Patton, the warehouse manager?"

"Oh no. So was that where she was going last night, to the warehouse to meet Ty?"

"I doubt it. She told Rachel she was meeting someone, and if it turned out well, she might be able to take off for Hollywood. So that wouldn't have been Ty. Ty's a good lookin' young guy, probably could go to Hollywood himself—but sure doesn't have any money if that's what she meant."

"Who has access to the warehouse besides Ty?" I asked.

"Just about anybody who works here. It would be pretty hard to get in there from the outside. Dun has it locked up tighter than a duck's ass: locks, cameras— the whole enchilada. But from inside it's easier. In short, anybody who works here could get in with their PIN tapped into the pad next to the door.

"Are the PINS assigned, or does everyone make up their own," I pressed.

"You don't need a PIN to get in if you're a customer. You'd only be going in there when it's open anyway."

Hmmm.

"I guess the police know all this, about Ty, right?"

"Hell, I don't know! What are you up to? You sound like you're prying. I told you messing with Dun could mean trouble for you," he scolded me.

"I don't know about you, but I have to get out of Wonderly as fast as I can, and if the police need some help, I think I should lend a hand," I persisted.

"I haven't been interviewed by the police, have you? They did say they were going to talk to everybody. God knows when we'll be able to get out of here. Maybe with the spring thaw."

"Precisely. That's why I'm going to try to move things along," I said, opening the bathroom door and tip-toeing out.

Oh, for God's sake, I was moist from all the steam in that bathroom.

CHAPTER 8

The thought of spring thaw didn't fill me with the usual feelings of ebullience that comes with a daffodil peeking through the snow. I had a serious mission now—not only was I inquisitive, but more importantly, I had to get back to my store.

Dashing back to 239 to splash some water on my face, I realized I sure could have used a short snooze. But lunch was about to be served, so I looked with dismay at my ruffled curls that didn't look half as good as Red Neck Ricky's. I went to lunch anyway.

Touchstone's *What About Bob?* trailer had already been sent to Annie's and was very popular. We all watched it at least once, Neil several times. So I wondered what kind of promotions Touchstone would have designed to market this video— a mini-therapist's couch?

I particularly loved the movie because my Moms and I had vacationed at Lake Winnipesaukee a few summers. The lake in the movie didn't look exactly like what I remembered, but it brought back magical memories of the three of us in a speedboat zipping around with Helen at the helm. My favorite exploit was one outing when Helen almost rammed into the dock while backing into the slip. Way too fast. Seeing Em jump in, screaming "throttle, throttle," and heaving the Titanic (as we laughingly called it) away from the dock, made a great vacation even better for a ten-year old.

Lunch wasn't designated seating, but Daisy, naturally, called me to her table. The clever centerpieces this time were "flowers" designed from aqua-colored DON'T HASSLE ME I'M LOCAL T-shirts like Bill Murray, as Bob, wore in the movie. The tote bag on my chair was filled with other free-bies: another T-shirt, a small pocketbook titled *Baby Steps,* a poster, and a mini-flashlight with *What About Bob?* inscribed on it in tiny letters. I hooked it over the back of my chair away from Daisy.

"Daisy, if I have to go to the restroom or leave for a few minutes, will you watch my bag?" Surely she'd get the hint that she shouldn't steal it.

At the front of the room stood Dun Wonderly and the Touchstone rep. The room was busy with chatter until Dun tapped the microphone with his hand a few times to get everybody's attention. "Good afternoon! Hope ya'll had a chance to visit the wonderful Wonderly Convention floor this mornin'."

Hoots and hollers from the tables ensued.

"Wail, I just wanna tell you I'm so dang sorry about you're not bein' able to leave tomorra that I've thought up a special treat."

Yeas and more hoots from the tables.

"A lottery is bein' set up for you folks to pick a numba. If your numba's called, you'll be comin' to ma house for dinner tomorra night. I sure as hail wish it could be everybody, but ya know, it's not the White House. Heh heh heh. Doors are openin' 'bout seven. Be there or be square. Heh heh heh."

"We haven't been questioned by the police yet, Dun. When's that going to happen?" someone called out.

"Wail, I believe Denny said that was startin' this evenin'. They had to finish in the warehouse, I'm told. So now without any more of my blabber-ing, here's Jody—he's a guy not a girl—heh, heh. Jody from Touchstone, take it away."

The *What About Bob?* trailer played to laughs and claps as one of the inside reps passed around a tub with numbers for the honor of supping with Dun. I picked 12, which is my lucky number, so I was feeling, yep, lucky.

Lunch was fried chicken, corn on the cob, and a salad—just like Bill Murray as Bob enjoyed at Dr. Leo Marvins' (played by Richard Dreyfuss) summer house on Lake Winnipesaukee. I didn't hear anybody moaning with delight as Bob had done in the movie, but replicating that dinner was a nice touch. The strawberry shortcake dessert was even better.

As we were getting up to leave, Dun took the mic again, "Now wait just a secon' there. Don't ya wanna know who's comin' to ma house for dinner? If I call your numba and you have a spouse or you're with someone, well then, they can come along, too. Here are the numbas…"

You guessed it, he picked number 12. Strangely, everybody else's number at the table was also picked except for Hermy's. Daisy's number was picked, but since she and Hermy were a couple, he was among the anointed. It almost seemed fixed. Why me? Could it have had something to do with room 237?

Fantasia was awaiting me after lunch, and I was looking forward to it. Even in a convention hall, Disney is bound to make an impression. Attendees were more sluggish after lunch, and the line to the floor was a lot slower with no pushing.

I gasped as I entered the convention floor—the Bare Bottom Babe had been defaced, literally. Her head cut off at the neck, leaving an unsightly jagged cardboard edge. It appears someone wanted to remain anonymous as promised. But I had to move on to *Fantasia*. I'd think about the decapitation later.

As expected, the Disney booth took up twice as much room as the other studios, and the huge Disney logo added to the wow factor. *Fantasia* was playing on an immense screen on laser disc. I didn't carry laser discs in my store, but I'd special order any title. There weren't enough customers who owned Laser Disc players to warrant stocking them. But *Fantasia* on laser disc was impressive; the animation and the sound were sparkling. You had to hand it to old Walt. Who would have thought ancient mythology set to a classical score would have enraptured children? But the eye-popping animation did the trick.

Our goody bags included a press kit announcing that after fifty days the VHS and LaserDisc would no longer be available. (Buy this classic now or it's gone forever!) Genius marketing. Also in the bag was a T-shirt with Mickey dressed as the Sorcerer's Apprentice and a pin with the same image.

The jagged green Bald Mountain with angry blue swirly skies loomed over the booth. I mean loomed. It started on the ceiling and curved halfway down to the floor on the canvas screen. This was the part of the movie that scared the bejesus out of my son Bogie when he was four.*

He much preferred Hyacinth Hippo dancing to Ponchielli's "Dance of the Hours."

That was one of my favorite parts, too, although I couldn't watch it without singing along to Allan Sherman's take, "Hello Muddah, Hello Fadduh." Classical shtick. And now that I think of it, Hyacinth's brief tutu was much like the Bare Bottom Babes standee's bit of fluffy tulle. Except nobody had lopped off Hyacinth's head as they had the Bare Bottom Babe's noggin.

---

* Bogie's name was really Humphrey. When I first saw *Casablanca,* and as I sat sobbing after the "Here's looking at you, kid" scene at the airport, I vowed I'd name my children Humphrey and Ingrid. Sadly, Bogie's friends call him "Hump," and Ingrid's friends call her "Grid." I call them Bogie and Iggy. Or Humphrey and Ingrid if I'm mad at them.

CHAPTER 9

Compared to the majesty of the *Fantasia* exhibit, the rest of the floor held no temptation. How could blank VHS tapes, shelving, or labels compare? They couldn't, so I climbed the stairs to 239 to organize my goody bags and my thoughts.

As I was sifting through all that I had gathered and cleaning out my handbag, I flipped through my little notebook and found the telephone number Jessica had scribbled down. I took it over to the table by the window, propped my feet up on the bed, and thought. Hmm. Should I call the number? Her family must be in horrible pain, but maybe I could find out something the police hadn't been able to. Surely they'd been interviewed. What is the worst that could happen? They'd kick me out as a heartless buttinsky? Well, I wasn't heartless, but maybe if they filled in some of the blanks, it would help me find out what happened to Jessica. And get me back to the store. How? I had no idea.

While procrastinating I straightened up to make the sad little room look at least neat. Finally I screwed my courage to the sticking place, picked up the phone, and tapped in Jessica's telephone number.

"Hello," answered a weak, quavery voice.

"Hi. My name is Annie Fillmore. I'm a customer of Wonderly Entertainment. Is this Jessica's mother?"

"Yes," she answered

"I had dinner with your beautiful daughter last evening before the horrible accident and wondered if you'd be interested in knowing what our conversation was about. I know this is a terrible, terrible time for you, and I wouldn't suggest it if I didn't think it might help to find out just what happened to Jessica last night."

Silence.

"Hello," I inquired.

"Yes, I'm here. I'm thinking. Can I call you back?" she said, hesitating.

"Of course," I answered, and gave her my number.

Dislodging the bedspread again with my two fingers, I noticed the Glade Air Freshener and was surprised that it did make the tiniest difference. Actually, I'm not sure if it covered the pall of tobacco, but the powdery aroma of the Country Pottery Air Freshener at least smelled clean.

I lay down and thought about what I knew had happened to Jessica and, maybe, Bobby Crane. I knew for sure that Jessica was meeting someone in the warehouse and was thinking about leaving Wonderly for Hollywood. Or that's what Rachel told Rob. I knew Bobby Crane met his end in room 237, but the reasons for both deaths remained a mystery. I didn't know for sure, but Bobby's death could have had something to do with the Bare Bottom Babes.

As I was running possible reasons through my head about Jessica, the phone rang.

"Hello?"

"Is this Miss Fillmore?" a voice asked.

"Yes, this is Annie."

"This is Alice Bostick, Jess's mother. You can come over if you still want to. We live in Wonderly Acres at the end of Pleasant Street. Do you know where that is?"

"Yes, I passed it on my way to the lake. What's the house number?"

"Fourth house on the right. It's got lots of flowers on the porch. You know, that people left here for Jess."

"Thank you, Mrs. Bostick. I'll walk over from the hotel. Not sure how long that will be, but I'm leaving now."

"Okay."

Luckily the drizzle had stopped and a pale sun fell on the flat concrete parking lot. What was here before this? A farm? Grazing sheep? Joni Mitchell's words played in my head, "…they paved paradise to put up a parking lot."

Heading down Pleasant Street again I saw it was a likable little town. Various colored awnings shaded the storefronts, and autumn flowers spilled out of pots by the front doors. The awnings were probably a necessity without trees to keep the sun off their front windows, fading their valuable goods. If I had anything but posters in my front window, I might have considered an awning, too.

I walked past Boo-Kay Florist and Tom's Pharmacy and stopped in front of Wittler's Antique Mall. Peeking in the window I saw that I could waste some good time in there. It was chockablock with anything anybody would want to own that they'd probably thrown away themselves years before. K & K Hardware was just as full to the brim including a dandy display of pumpkins of every size.

Delilah's Candies was next to K & K, and I decided to stop for some candy to bring to Jessica's mother. Flowers would apparently be redundant. Delilah's smelled inviting as I opened the door to a chocolate delight. My feet creaked on the old wooden floor, alerting someone in the back that they had a customer. The counter displayed baskets of all different kinds of candies covered with clear cellophane and closed with showy bows. I had to peek through them to see the clerk standing on the other side.

"Hi, I'm looking for something to bring Mrs. Bostick whose daughter Jessica passed away yesterday," I said, figuring everyone in town knew about it, and why not say it out loud.

"How nice of you. Sure, any one of these baskets on display would be good," she answered in a lovely drawl.

"These look more for celebration than mourning. Perhaps something less showy?" I asked.

"Oh maybe," she said, pointing to the wall where boxes of chocolates and other candies were displayed.

"I'll take the Godiva Mixed Chocolates. The fifteen piece."

With my Delilah's Candies bag in hand I hurried on down the street, passing The Wonder Restaurant, Finery Boutique, Derby Saddlery, and then I stopped looking at stores and hurried on to Wonderly Acres.

Jessica's porch was scattered with bouquets of flowers, a few teddy bears, and a sign that said we love you Jess. This was going to be hard, but something pushed me up those two steps as I tried to avoid stepping on Jessica's memorial flowers.

A lump lodged in my throat, and tears welled up in my eyes as I approached the front door. I took a deep breath, slapped myself in the face lightly, and silently said this woman just lost her daughter. Stop it. Now. When I had stemmed my emotions, I rang the doorbell.

Alice Bostick opened the door slowly, looking withered. She was beautiful in the same way as Jessica was, but she looked defeated. Her jeans and green T-shirt were pressed, but her hair hadn't seen a brush.

"Hi, Mrs. Bostick, I'm Annie Fillmore. We spoke on the phone?"

"Yes. Come on in," she said, motioning.

The living room was as ironed and neat as Alice's shirt and jeans. A blue couch and matching chairs faced a large TV, accented by a blue-patterned rug. The walls were hung with photos of Jessica from the time she was a baby until recently.

I handed her the box of candy, but didn't say anything. I didn't know what to say.

"How kind," she said, taking the candy and placing it on a glass coffee table in front of the couch. "Please sit. Can I get you coffee or tea or a pop?"

"Thank you, a glass of water would be great. But I don't want to put you to any trouble," I said.

"No trouble. I need to do something besides sit here and cry. I have lots of people coming over in about a half hour, but I wanted to hear what you had to say before they got here."

She walked to the kitchen area, which was separated from the living room by a short counter. It looked like they'd moved in the day before— everything was spotless and new.

"Did you just move here?" I asked.

"No. We've been here since Jess was born. Well, I'm here now. Her Papa and I divorced about ten years ago, so it's just me and Jessica. I mean...." She didn't finish.

She brought me a glass of water in a fancy amber goblet. "So tell me what Jess had to say to you last night."

I told her everything Jessica had told me. I also mentioned that I had found the police outline of a body in room 237, which I suspected was where Bobby Crane died. And I thought I saw Jessica run under the staircase to the warehouse and office area at about ten forty-five.

She sat staring at her hands that she fidgeted with in her lap. "Did you meet Ty?" she questioned, not looking up.

"No. I think I may have seen him at The Wonder in the bar before Jessica joined me, but we didn't meet."

"They've been together since they were freshmen in high school. He lives just down the street, so they've known each other since his family, the Pattons, moved here from a few towns over when he was in third grade— when he and Jess were in third grade."

"He must be as devastated as you," I said, not having a clue who could be more devastated than a mother losing a child.

She looked up from her lap. "He took off this morning. Left me a note under my door that said, 'I might be next. I'm getting out of here.'"

The hairs on my neck stood at attention. "Do you have any idea what he could mean by that?" I asked almost breathless.

"No idea at all. I know he and Jess wanted to leave Wonderly and set out for California when they saved enough money. It's funny how when you don't like a place, people always say, 'Well, just leave.' How? How do you leave if you don't have the money to leave? This town was fine when Jess was in school, but now, what's the point of being here?"

I commiserated with her, but before her friends arrived I wanted to steer her back to what Ty could possibly have meant by that note.

"The police will no doubt want to talk to Ty, seeing as they were so close and he was the warehouse manager, don't you think?" I asked.

"Yes, they want to talk to him, but he doesn't want to talk to them. He wouldn't take off at a time like this if he wasn't scared. Really scared. I just wish I knew what could spook him so much. I mean besides Jess being dead. He must think she was killed instead of being in an accident as Mr. Wonderly said this morning when he called."

"Mr. Wonderly called you this morning? What did he say if I may ask?"

"Just that. He said he was powerful sorry to have to tell me the news, but Jess was killed in an accident in the warehouse when she was climbing up a shelf to get a video, and that he'd do anything he could to help me. Whatever I need, I should just ask," she replied.

"Do you think Ty will be in touch with you from wherever he is? Surely he'll want to know the outcome of the investigation. In a meeting this morning the police chief said they were investigating whether Jessica's death was an accident or something else. He must have meant if she had been killed."

"It certainly makes no sense at all that Jess would climb that shelving at ten-forty-five at night. She knew enough not to do something as stupid as that in broad daylight even. That's a crock. But what she *was* doing there, I have no idea," Alice related.

"Last year there was a murder in my town that I helped the police solve. Well, I didn't actually work with the police, I kind of worked behind their backs; but I sure would love to get to the bottom of what happened to Jess and this Bobby Crane. I think I have a knack for sleuthing, as crazy as that sounds."

"Whatever you can do to help would be appreciated. It won't bring Jess back, but she could at least rest in peace. Let me know if there is anything I can do to help," she said, getting up from her chair.

"Are you in touch with Ty's family?" I prodded, still sitting.

She sat down again.

"Ty's mom passed when he was, gosh, I think, in sixth grade. His dad isn't much good these days. Lost himself in a bottle from grief and never did get his head out, so Ty takes care of him, not the other way around like you'd think." She stood up once more.

"Okay. I have your number and you have mine. I'll let you know what I find out, and please let me know if Ty gets in touch with you. He probably holds the key, don't you think?"

"It sounds like it. Poor guy. He's like a son to me after all these years, so right now I've lost a daughter and a son. He was truly part of our little family," she said on a sob.

We hugged good-bye. Actually, I hugged her, and as I opened the door, I saw cars pulling up and a few people coming down the street on foot. I nodded at them in mutual mourning and made my way back to The Dunbar.

I was sad…and hungry. I wished I'd bought some of that chocolate for me to tide me over.

CHAPTER 10

By the time I was halfway back to the hotel, the sun was shining brightly on Wonderly despite the mantle of sadness at the loss of Jessica Bostick's life.

A little rest was needed before I attended Marketing Magic with Mark Heyward, a supposed marketing guru. I also needed to shop in the warehouse for sale videos. And when would I be slated to speak with Chief Denny Earl? What would we talk about? I guess I'd let him ask me questions—I learned that much from Detective Tom Ward in Cincinnati during my caper with crime last year.

As I climbed the two short flights of stairs, I realized I was more than tired. I was drained. More than likely I was emotionally weary from the reality of Jessica's tragic death and seeing up close a mother's worst fear of losing a child. A nap was in order for sure, even though I should have gone back to the convention floor to look for computer software and stuff.

As I opened the door I was surprised to see a bouquet of flowers next to the TV. Then I saw him. He was stretched out on the bed by the window, hands behind his head, looking like he belonged.

"What are you doing here? And how did you get in?" I asked Neil.

"Hi to you, too," he replied.

"How did you get into my room?" I really *was* curious.

"Hope you don't mind, but I told them at the desk I was your son and I wanted to surprise you."

"You're Indian. We don't even look like we're from the same continent. My son? And what a compliment to think you're young enough to be my son. What about the next question; what are you doing here?"

"Did you notice the flowers I brought you? I'm on the woo."

I did have to smile to myself. On the woo. I'd never heard that expression before, but I knew what he meant.

"You cut quite the gallant figure lying on my bed with your big toe sticking out of your sock, Casanova," I said.

"I wanted to surprise you, and it sounded like you needed company."

I kicked off my shoes, smelled the flowers that didn't smell, removed the bedspread from the other bed, and lay down.

"Thank you for the flowers, they're lovely and smell delicious, and it *is* good to see a familiar face," I said, turning toward him. "But you can't stay in this room tonight if that's what you're thinking."

"I figured if you had two beds I could sleep in one; not in your bed, not together."

"No. Sorry, you can't stay here, and I doubt if there are any rooms available; this place is packed with video store owners. But there's a dinner and a show tonight, let me see if it's okay if you come with me to that—if you want to stay that late."

"Brilliant," he said. "Have you seen many celebrities?"

"Red Neck Ricky, if you'd call him a celebrity."

"What, the wrestling guy? That's the only celebrity you've seen?"

"Yep. I need to take a nap. You can stay here while I nap, but then you have to find a place to stay unless you're driving back tonight. "

"I'm staying," he said curtly.

"Ok. Do you have anything to wear to dinner? A jacket?"

"No, but I saw a men's shop on the way in. I'll check there."

"That might be kind of pricey. There's probably a used clothing shop in town."

Then I fell asleep.

A gentle nudge woke me up. "Annie, it's three fifty. Do you need to go to that marketing thing at four that's on the schedule?" Neil asked.

"Oh shit," I said in my best ladylike vernacular.

"Sorry I didn't wake you sooner. I fell asleep, too," he apologized.

"It's not your fault, sweetie, uh, Neil."

Shoving my feet in my shoes, I looked in the mirror on the way out the door and saw that my hair looked like I'd stuck my finger in an electric socket—it was a huge, standing-on-end mess.

I sprinted to room 2 to learn marketing tips to make Annie's Video and Music Hall profitable, a meeting that seemed worthwhile.

The room was almost full when I tiptoed in, but I caught the eye of a burly guy in the front. "Come on down!" he said in a good imitation of Bob Barker. "I've been saving a seat for you up front," he gestured toward an empty seat in the front row.

Oh geez. Slinking down the aisle I tried not to make eye contact with him, but it was hard because I could feel him looking at me, or maybe it was just my hair.

"We've all introduced ourselves, so let's find out who the latecomer is," he said in what I thought I recognized as a New Jersey accent.

"I'm Annie Fillmore from Annie's Video and Music Hall."

"What a great name for a store–a Woody Allen fan?" he said in a wonderful hearty voice.

I stared at him for a second, wow… not many people recognized that. This *was* going to be an interesting hour or so.

He turned to a huge whiteboard in the front of the room. "Okay, let's get started," he boomed.

"Number one, and the only marketing tool for every business you can think of…" and he wrote down: you work for the customer.

"The only difference between you and your competitors is you. That's right, the way you and your staff treat your customers is the difference between say, 'Annie's Video and Music Hall' and 'Video Ventures' down the street. We can talk about this for the full hour, but there are hundreds of ways to stand out with customers, so let's talk about a few."

The hour flew by with profit-making suggestions from Heyward. We found out in the course of his delivery he owned three stores in New Jersey that were all thriving. The biggest takeaways were: know your customers by name, give them something special every once in a while (like swag you received from the studios), and forgive late fees for your best customers.

When Heyward mentioned giving away studio swag to customers, Daisy Dixon raised her hand.

"We *sell* our customers the giveaways. They're happy and we make some money," she said with a bit of swagger.

"Well, in New Jersey we'd call that kind of chintzy," Heyward responded with a laugh.

After the question-and-answer segment of the presentation, we all applauded.

As I was leaving, he pulled me aside and asked, "Do you belong to the VSDA in your area?"

"No. I've been asked, but I'm not sure what it's all about aside from protecting stores that carry X-rated videos."

"It's much more than that. It's a way of having a voice with the studios and the upcoming insurgence of Blockbuster. Blockbuster is a monster that will surely give Mom and Pops a run for their money. We can use all the people we can get to stand up to what will be an uneven playing field."

Hmm. And here I thought I'd go into my golden years owning a video store.

"Thanks, Mark. I'll join when I get back home. If I get back home. Do you have to stay to be interviewed by the police, too?"

"No, I arrived this morning and will be leaving this evening, so I escaped an interrogation. Here's my card. Call me if you want to chat about the video business. I've been in it from day one and love it and want to see it continue as long as possible."

Whatever it was about this guy, I liked him. You can tell genuine. Okay, I can't always tell genuine; I've been suckered quite a few times, but Mark Heyward was the real deal.

Daisy was waiting for me at the end of the hallway. "You're from New York aren't you?" she asked.

"Yes."

"What does chintzy mean?" she asked, brows knitted.

"Clever. It means clever, Daisy." I wasn't about to tell her it meant cheap in New Jersey.

"That's what I thought," she said beaming.

And off she went, thinking she was clever instead of cheap.

Four fifteen would give me enough time to check out the warehouse and buy some sale videos. My list of what I wanted to purchase was back in the room, but I thought I could remember most of them. At the top of the list was the Coen Brothers' *Miller's Crossing* that a customer rented and then kept for his very own. We had another copy, but its popularity warranted two. And, of course, it was one of the store's favorites. We also needed a few Disney tapes that are always in demand. I wasn't sure if the ones I wanted were on Moratorium. That's a Disney term meaning they take certain titles out of circulation to build up fervor for their re-release. I saved all of these orders for the convention instead of ordering over the phone—every dollar saved means more videos.

I followed the signs to the warehouse, winding my way through the cubicles where the inside sales reps sat. The young woman standing sentry at the door to the seemingly endless shelves of videos wore a name tag that said LINDA CHAMBERS. Was this my rep, Linda, I wondered?

"Linda? Annie Fillmore," I said.

"Oh! I've been looking for you, but with all of my other customers I've been busy." We hugged like two women who talk on the phone every day—which we do.

"It's great to meet you finally, but what a terrible time for all of you," I sympathized.

"The worst. We were all pretty close, some closer than others, but Jess and I were tight. I still can't wrap my head around it. It makes no sense," she said, her voice faltering. "She would never climb those shelves to get a video, she knew better than that. And there are grabbers if you can't reach; we all use them. But she did have a video in her hand when she was found … at least that's what I heard."

"What was the video?" I pried.

"Why? Does it matter?" She questioned.

"Just curious."

She looked at me warily. "That's right, you did tell me about the murder last year up by your store, right?"

"Yes. And from every book I've read or movie I've seen, the truth is always in the details. Can you find out what the video was?"

"I don't know how, but I guess I can try. Oh, do you know that Jess's boyfriend is missing? He's the warehouse manager, and nobody knows where he's at. Don't you think that's suspicious? But there's no way Ty would hurt Jess. She was his north star."

I didn't let on that I knew about Ty or that I met Jessica's mom. I was going to let her tell me what she knew first.

"So your desks are just outside the warehouse?" I asked.

"Yes. Easy access when a customer wants to know what's in stock. Why don't you shop? It's almost time to close up; then I'll take you for a little tour."

I found the Twentieth Century Fox section and retrieved a copy of *Miller's Crossing*. Just holding it my hand made me happy. I first discovered the Coen Brothers with *Blood Simple* and fell in love with them with *Raising Arizona*. *Miller's Crossing* is a perfect example of why I love movies. The opening credits with the mournful music playing against the canopy of trees and the black hat fluttering along the forest floor still sends chills. It might be one of my favorite openings of a movie. Oh, who am I kidding; it's just among the hundreds that bring me joy.

Instead of shopping, I edged my way to a huge canvas curtain that separated the open warehouse from the crime scene. I went over to the last shelf next to the hanging canvas, and looked over my shoulder to see if Linda was watching me. The aisles between the shelves were wide—wide enough for someone strong to push one over. I so wanted to peek behind the heavy curtain, but it was dark back there and I wasn't sure I could see anything anyway…but also, I didn't want Linda to think I was doing exactly what I was told not to do.

"Annie? Where are you?" Linda called out.

"I'm over here. Where are the Bare Bottom Babes videos shelved?" I asked innocently.

"Oh yeah. Those were on the shelf that fell over. Those and the Wet T-Shirt videos. Do you want one? Doesn't sound like something you usually stock."

"No, but Playboy and Penthouse videos are always out, so these may make me a few dollars. Have they been moved to another area of the warehouse? I'd like to buy one and play it in my room upstairs to see if it's something I want to add to my MIDNGHT section."

"I have a copy that's opened if you want to check it out. I'm closing the warehouse for the day. I doubt anybody else is going to be shopping at this hour. Come on, I'll give you the tour."

She shut off the lights in the warehouse, heaved closed the massive door on rollers, and entered her number in the PIN pad, 45831. I silently repeated it to myself over and over to commit it to memory.

"Here it is, our luxurious office," she said, sweeping her arm out as if she were showcasing a winning prize.

The false ceiling was low and dimpled, and the glaring fluorescent lights weren't filtered. It made me think of a police interrogation room. Were there two-way mirrors, too?

The worn grey carpet looked as seedy as my hotel room carpet, and the white walls were yellowing. The girls had each prettied up their cubes with lamps, family photos, some kids' art work, and one even wallpapered the inside of her cubicle.

"Come on. I'll show you where the king lives," she said, nudging me and winking.

In the middle of the right wall was a large ornate wooden door carved with flowers, curlicues, and birds. Linda pulled down on a fancy brass lever and opened the door to reveal a wide hallway carpeted in black and gold.

The carpet color scheme was duplicated on a huge gaudy cabinet taking up most of the left wall.

"What's in that cabinet?" I probed.

"We're getting up to date by computerizing our customer files. Check this out," she said pulling out a file drawer. "Every video store in the country is included in this card catalog. Our customers are on blue cards; those who aren't currently our customers are on yellow cards. It's a bitch entering all this into the computer, but we have to do it every day until we're done."

The right wall displayed photos of Dun and celebrities. A spotlight shined on a photo of Dun and another guy shaking hands. "What's going on here?" I asked Linda.

"That's Dun with the governor of Kentucky the night Dun was commissioned as a member of The Honorable Order of Kentucky Colonels."

"That sounds pretty important," I said.

"Yeah, I guess. It's a charitable organization and pretty much means you can donate to causes that benefit the people of Kentucky. But it's an honor to be asked.

Wait 'til you see the throne room." Linda giggled.

She opened another embellished door on the right and flicked the light switch to show something you might expect for royalty. It was positively vulgarian. Aside from the wooden desk with inlaid motifs, everything in the room was gold or trimmed with gold. Did this guy have a gold toilet seat, too?

On the wall behind Dun's desk, two rifles were mounted on a gold gun rack. The rifles were old and didn't go with the deluxe rack, but there's no accounting for taste, as this room testified.

"Does Dun collect rifles?" I inquired, walking toward them to have a closer look and to feel the wood.

"Eeek. Don't touch the wood handle. Marla, the girl who cleans his office, wears extra sturdy rubber gloves because she got terrible splinters when she first started dusting what Dun calls his Kentucky Long Rifles. He says these belonged to Daniel Boone, but who knows if that's true. They look old enough though. But check this out. Here's the only part I'd actually want in my house," she said moving across the big room. She slid around the desk to a door with a small window on the back wall. "Ta Da," she announced when she opened the door by its golden U-shaped handle to reveal a steam room—a luxury steam room that included a grey tile chaise lounge plus another ledge, perhaps to lie down flat. Holy smokes, I wanted one of those, too.

"That's it. What do you think?" she asked.

"Kind of yuck except for the steam room."

"Yeah, way over the top for me, too. Let me get you the copy of Bare Bottom Babes to see if you want to stock them. Then I have to get going; I'm one of the hosts for cocktails and dinner tonight, and I have to run home to shower and get dressed."

"I hope it's not fancy, I only brought one all-purpose black dress," I said.

"That'll be fine. You never know with this bunch what people will wear—overalls to lamé.

We parted with another hug, and I climbed the stairs to paradise in room 239. I wondered if Neil would be back from his shopping and hoped he would be, even though I didn't want to hope he would be.

CHAPTER 11

And there he was, standing in front of the mirror checking himself out in his thrift store purchase. He was wearing a tuxedo jacket with rounded satin lapels, a white shirt, and a black bow tie. His pants and shoes were the ones he had on when he arrived earlier that day.

"How formal. How dapper," I said appreciatively.

"Blinding or cock-up?" he asked.

"If blinding means good, you're blinding, Ringo. You'll be perfect. Linda told me people wear everything from overalls to lamé—and you seem to have them both covered."

"Yeah, they didn't have the pants to go with the jacket, but I figured once they saw the jacket they wouldn't pay attention to the bottom."

"I'll call down to ask Rob if it's okay, but I'm sure it is. You'll be a feast for the eyes of all those beautiful young women."

"I'll only have eyes for you," he answered.

He *was* on the woo!

"I'm going to pop in the shower and then iron my wrinkled dress."

"Oops, I think I used all the towels. They're not that thick, so I used them all."

Luckily I had time to call down for more towels, call Rob to get his okay for Neil, and iron my dress.

"Towels," a voice said with a knock on the door.

A short woman in a raspberry uniform with a name tag that said ROSA appeared at the door.

Rosa, that's the name of the woman who saw the dead body.

"Hi, Rosa. Thank you so much for coming up at such a busy time. Please come in," I said, motioning for her to come in with the wave of my arm. Then I clicked on the TV and turned it to the highest volume just in case Rob was right and the room was bugged.

"Oh, no no. I cannot." But she did step into the room.

"Please. I want to give you a tip for bringing the towels, and I also wanted to ask you about the man in two thirty-seven. I was in that room, too. It was frightening, wasn't it?"

"No, no," she responded.

"I just want to ask you a few questions, and I promise (I crossed my heart and put my hands in prayer mode) I won't say a word to anyone. I promise." I zipped my lips and threw away a pretend key. If she didn't understand what that meant, she no doubt thought I was a crazy lady.

She looked at me and turned to look at Neil, who looked pretty swanky in his second-hand duds. She might have thought he was reason enough to talk, a good-looking guy can do that to a woman.

"No," she said.

"I just want to know when you saw him and when he disappeared."

She looked at me and Neil again and again. She must have been sizing us up to decide whether she should say another word, especially after the reps told her to be quiet, for her own good.

Neil nodded his head at her and in his deep sexy voice said, "It's okay, Rosa. You're safe here."

"I see his body on Thursday, but not on Friday. On Friday he's gone."

"What time did you see his body on Thursday?" I prodded.

She looked again at Neil, and again Neil nodded his assent.

"In morning, when I clean the rooms. When I knock, no answer. I opened the door and find him. I am so scared I don't know what to do. Mr. Dun gets mad quick. I called my boss, Miss Maria. She tells me to leave and be quiet. But somebody knows I saw him, a girl at the desk downstairs. She said be quiet. So I'm quiet."

"Did you go into the room again the next day?"

"Yes, for momento, but I see a chalk body, and leave."

"You are very brave, Rosa," I said, reaching into my wallet for a twenty-dollar bill. She didn't look at it when I gave it to her. She just said, "I go now."

When the door closed behind her, I stood with my back resting on it like an old movie star does when the romantic interest leaves.

"That was fucking great," Neil said. "You're like Miss Marple and I'm like Columbo."

"You've got the age difference about right," I commented, raising my eyebrows.

"Are you kidding? I got excited just seeing you in action. Did you get hot seeing me?"

Who wouldn't?

"I was trying to get information from her, and we succeeded. Thank you for doing your bit. You were perfect."

"Does that deserve a kiss?" he asked, cocking his head.

"It deserves a shower," I cautioned.

"Together?"

"Uh, no."

Rob said of course I could bring Neil. They knew each other from the store, and even though it might have seemed like they were from different planets to a casual passerby, they were both smart and funny. I think they would have become friends after a beer or two.

I took my shower, and put on my black dress. After our impromptu interrogation of Rosa, I didn't have time to iron it. I stepped into some nude heels, tossed on some gold dangly earrings and a long gold necklace. I'd already curled my already curly hair with my curling iron. I know it sounds weird to curl curly hair, but it works for me. Everything I was wearing was a tad damp, since I'd had to bring my clothes into the bathroom. There *was* a peeping Tom in my room after all.

When I stepped out of the bathroom, Neil was standing against the opposite wall with his arms crossed, and he did the Eartha Kitt purr I'd heard him do before...not for me, but for whatever femme fatale movie star he thought was sexy. So hearing it for me, well.... He definitely could not stay in the room with me in the next bed. Definitely not.

"We've got about fifteen minutes for cocktails to start, and I don't like to be the first to arrive— let's take a walk, or at least get some fresh air, okay?" I offered.

"Let's do it," he obliged.

Walking down the stairs to the lobby, Neil grabbed my hand. I looked up at him. "To steady you on the stairs," he said not looking at me.

Blimey, there was what felt like an electric current running up my arm.

The light mizzle outside of the hotel prevented us from taking a walk, so we stood under the overhang and breathed in the dead parking lot air infused with a hint of bourbon.

"What can I expect tonight? I'm not great about the social mixing," Neil admitted.

"What? You'll be fine. You're so good with the customers at the store. I don't know many people either. Just say hello; they'll more than likely say the rest." I soothed.

"I'm fine when there's a counter between us, but otherwise not so much," he confessed.

Mid-conversation, a red Corvette convertible zoomed up in front of us with a squeal and pulled into the no-parking zone just to our right. The vanity plate said, WONDER. The owner hopped out, looking the picture of a country gentleman in a brown tweed jacket with matching vest, a light grey shirt, and blue jeans. He nodded at us as he passed. I said, "Hi," and then to Neil, "That must be Dun Wonderly's brother, who owns the restaurant where I had dinner with Jessica last night."

"If you like that type," Neil responded.

I ignored him.

"A Corvette ZR-1," Neil instructed.

"Huh?" I responded.

"That's the make of the car. Nice. I guess he doesn't mind getting his pomaded hair wet in the rain."

"I guess not." From the short glimpse I'd had of him, he and his brother didn't look alike. He was much younger for starters, and way better dressed. Maybe different mothers?

"We can think about going in now, but I forgot to ask where you're staying tonight."

"Check this out. There's a lower floor in the hotel with a huge pool with rooms around it. Don't know who'd want to stay in those rooms, the smell of chlorine might kill them by morning, but I'll bring a towel to cover my face," he said.

"You got a room down there?" I asked, surprised.

"No, I pulled over one of the pool lounge chairs into a dark corner. I'm gonna sleep there."

"Okay. Take a pillow and a blanket from the other bed," I offered. I was a veritable Mother Teresa.

"It's hot down there; or at least it was this afternoon. But maybe it'll keep out the chlorine fumes that may or may not kill me."

Leapin' Lizards Lounge was hopping by the time we arrived at six fifteen.

Like the night before, there was a mish-mash of clothing styles just as Linda predicted–sequins to baggy jeans. Daisy's scanner was apparently at full throttle because I saw her hand waving at me through the throng. She dragged Hermy behind as she made her way over to me and Neil.

"I'll get us a drink," Neil said, taking off for the bar before Daisy and Hermy got to me.

"Did you notice it's a full bar tonight? Not just wine and beer. That Dun is so generous," Daisy gushed.

"Isn't this sponsored by Columbia? Dun sponsored last night with the beer and wine," I said. Why did I have to burst her Dun bubble?

"Either way. Even the waiters are in tuxes–that's pretty classy," she murmured.

Waiters in tuxedos? Uh oh, Daisy thought Neil was a waiter.

Neil came back and handed me a Scotch on the rocks, bless his heart. He was just about to take a sip of his wine when Daisy said to him, "I'll have a martini and Hermy. . . Hermy, what will you have?"

"Beer," said Hermy. "I'll get them."

"Oh no, this handsome waiter is getting it for us. A martini and a beer, please," she said, turning to Neil.

Neil just looked at her.

"Daisy, Hermy, I'd like you to meet, Neil Jakhar, my music buyer."

Neil shook Hermy's hand and nodded at Daisy.

"Oh, my goodness. You look like a waiter," Daisy said to him.

"Many thanks," Neil said bowing slightly.

"We've been so busy," Daisy said. "Have you been on the tour of the bourbon distillery?"

"No, I haven't. I didn't realize they have tours. If I'm here long enough, I guess I'll do that."

"Hmm," Neil said, "maybe I should stay."

The cocktail hour passed without further event, or almost no event. Rob came over and greeted us, as did Mayo, and Mr. Chicken Video.

At one point I looked up and saw Dun Wonderly staring at me. Every time I turned in his direction he seemed to be looking my way. Finally, he came over to our little group and took me aside. "I unnastand you had dinna with poor Jessica last naht," he said, standing way too close to me.

Backing up slightly, I told him I had.

"Why? Why did you have dinna with her? She's not a rep," he said narrowing his eyes at me.

"Is there a law down here about who you can have dinner with?" I asked, arching an eyebrow.

"Wail, no, cos not. Jus' curious why you would, since you don' know her."

"I was dining at Wonder when I saw her in the bar crying. You fired her yesterday, you may recall, because she gave me the key to room two thirty-seven instead of two thirty-nine, so I asked her to join me for dinner."

"Wail, now ah din't actually fya her. Ol' Dun gets his danda up once in a while, and that's what happens. I don' want ma guests stayin' in rooms that ahen't safe. I was thinkin' of you, not her. I went wrong, I admit it. She shoulda known I din't mean fovea—jus' a day or two until I cooled down."

I didn't respond.

"Jus' stopped by to say enjoy you're evenin'," he continued, then turned and went back across the room to mingle.

I took a breath and looked up to see Neil being escorted away by one of Wonderly's lovely reps. My heart sank. I hate that feeling of disappointment.

While I was stewing in my regret, Chicken Video came over to chat some more, and I realized everything we had to say to each other had been said on the line for *City Slickers*. Of course I was cordial, but I wasn't fascinated to know how much he raked in last week. He definitely needed that thrifty sign if what he raked in was $115.

Without trying to be too obvious, I turned again to see if I could spot Neil. My imagination had him bending that girl backward in a romantic kiss, but what I saw instead was Neil coming toward me balancing two plates and his wine.

"Where's your girlfriend?" I asked, peevishly.

"My girlfriend?"

"The girl who spirited you away," I whined.

"Jesus, for someone who's an adult—or supposed to be an adult–you act like a teenager sometimes."

Sadly, he nailed it.

Chicken Video walked away having enough sense not to listen to me act like an idiot. He might have made only $115 last week, but chances are he was smarter with his woman than I was with, well, whatever Neil was to me.

CHAPTER 12

Seven o'clock was nearing, and conventioneers were filtering out of Leapin' Lizards Lounge toward room 1 and our Fantasia Dinner.

From down the hall you could hear exclamations of delight from people who had already entered. No wonder. Neil and I walked into the room, which was bathed in a pale purplish hue. The deep purple tablecloths complemented the magical aura. The walls were replete with moving scenes from the fantastic movie. Sumptuous arrangements burst from the tables with flowers, vegetables, and wine-purple grapes. Fairy lights kindled each magnificent plume. Oh my, it was wonderful.

Daisy, as usual, was already at a table and waving her arms for us to join her, but Neil took my elbow and steered me to another table. He bent down to whisper, "We're not sitting with her. In the lounge she told me about an ear infection she had that when she bent over, dark fluid leaked out. No way do I want to hear any more of that."

There was only one other couple at the table Neil chose, and we introduced ourselves. Our tablemates were George and Amanda Carrington, who said they owned four video stores in Cincinnati. That sure sounded like a lot to me. They were seemingly of the manner born and quite a departure from me and Chicken Video. Bucky Henderson soon joined us, along with Linda Chambers, my inside rep, and two other Wonderly staff.

Bucky was fiddling with black-rimmed glasses that I hadn't noticed before, and I was wondering how long it was going to take before he introduced himself to me again. "Well, how about this for a fancy dinner?" he asked proudly.

"Michael always does it up right," commented Amanda Carrington.

Michael? If she was talking about Michael Eisner, the CEO of Disney, I doubt very much if he was in the kitchen stirring up the stew, or even contributing to the impressive purple mise-en-scène.

"How about everybody introduces themselves so we can have a good chat while we enjoy our dinner," said Bucky, who was dressed in khakis and a blue blazer with his blond hair looking even more perfect than the day before.

The Carringtons went first and told us about their four *very* large Video Estate stores in Cincinnati. Luckily, none of them were close to Annie's Video and Music Hall because, to hear them tell it, they were eating up the competition.

I told them about Annie's in short order, Linda informed them that she was an inside rep, Grant Hudson introduced himself as Wonderly's human resources director, and Charles Hammer was manager of Wonderly Entertainment's outlet in Indianapolis. When they started to serve us our impressive dinner of lobster tail and round steak, I stopped listening.

"What's happening with the investigation of that young woman's death?" asked George Carrington.

"Please, let's not bring up unpleasantness at this festive dinner," responded Bucky.

"Just wondering if it's being considered an accident or murder."

Bucky and the other Wonderly people ignored the question, but Neil blurted out, "And what about the dead guy in room two thirty-seven?"

He heaved to the right when I banged his thigh with mine under the table, and he turned to look at me. My eyes widened, signaling him to shut up, and I guess he got the point, because he did.

"There was nobody in room two thirty-seven. That's a rumor going around. There was a plumbing situation that made the room uninhabitable. That's all. Leave it to the tongue waggers to start a flap," Bucky said, chuckling.

Of course, it was no laughing matter. Rosa saw the body. I saw the results. To be polite I went along with Bucky's bad plumbing story. But I knew better.

Neil and I found seats third row center for The Bluegrass Pickers in the Wonderly Arena.

"I wish I had seats this great for someone I wanted to hear," he said, bending, whispering in my ear.

"How do you know you're not going to like them before you even hear them?"

"Just a hunch."

When the curtains parted, four men and one woman were on stage and started to play *Foggy Mountain Breakdown*, drowning out the enthusiastic applause. The group consisted of banjo, guitar, mandolin, and upright bass. The woman was on fiddle.

Rousing is how I'd describe it: toe-tapping, knee-slapping. Their fingers flew over the strings so fast I could hardly keep up with my eyes. I heard Neil murmur a soft "Wow."

I think we were both slightly bowled over at how much we enjoyed it. Nothing better than live music, even if you don't think you're going to like it. It put us both in quite an upbeat mood. Maybe too upbeat.

The rush out of the arena through the lobby to the stairs to my room took much less time than it should have. When we got to the door, I realized I'd left my purse somewhere. Neil pulled out the key that the clerk had ever so obligingly given him, not knowing if he could have been a murderer and *not* my son.

"I have to get my purse," I said half-heartedly.

"We'll get it," he said, opening the door, allowing me to go first. No sooner were we in the room than he moved me up against the wall, and we started kissing. Feverishly. I have no idea how long that went on because I felt like I was in another world, where kissing was breathing. He took my hand, leading me over to one of the beds when a loud knocking on the door stopped us mid-step.

"Go to the bathroom," I whispered.

He looked dazed, but did as I asked. I can't blame him, I was dazed, too.

Rob was standing at the door with my purse dangling from his raised finger. "Forget something?" he asked.

"Oh, my gosh. Thanks so much."

"How'd ya get in to your room without a key?" he asked.

"It's a long story," I mumbled.

"Can't be that long, the concert's only been over for about fifteen minutes."

"Anyway, thank you. I was just on my way out to look for it, but now I'm going to sleep," I said as I closed the door.

I've forgotten my purse so many times, sometimes it makes me wonder if my head is actually attached as my Uncle Fred often wondered aloud. But this time was the worst. So far.

Neil came out of the bathroom. He was rumpled, and I looked down to see that I was a mess, too.

"That sucked," Neil observed.

Indeed.

"But it might have been for the best. You should get your things and get ready to sleep by the pool. You have to drive home tomorrow, so you'll need some rest," I countered.

"Oh yeah, that's just what I need, sleep," he more or less moaned.

As I pulled the blanket and pillow off the bed, I'm not sure I've ever been more conflicted. Was I doing the right thing or being a fool?

I handed him the pillow and blanket. I didn't even give him a peck on the cheek to send him off to what I hoped wasn't a chlorine-induced coma.

CHAPTER 13

Even though I was exhausted, I had to check in with the store. I needed to hear things were okay.

"Hi, Kelly."

"Annie, hi. How are you? Neil told us about the murder, or maybe murders down there."

"Yeah, death seems to be following me. But how'd it go tonight?"

"Numbers were good, but your friend Sophie got into it with one of the customers."

"What? Oh no. A good customer?"

"No. I never saw her before. She wanted to sign up, but she didn't have a license or any other photo ID. Sophie was waiting on her and told her to come back with an ID or get lost."

"That doesn't sound too bad," I said hopefully.

"Oh, that's not all."

"The customer asked for Sophie's name, and Sophie told her it was none of her fucking business."

"Uh oh."

"Yeah. Then the customer reached her hand out and grabbed Sophie's sweater and pulled on it across the counter."

"Oh, my God."

"Sophie let her have it. Chopped the customer's hand off the sweater and took a swing at her."

"Good grief."

"Luckily, Mr. Swinton was in the store. You know him, the cop from Dunlop?"

"Oh, right. Did he break it up?"

"He asked the customer to leave the store, and he said to Sophie, 'It's none of your fucking business' might not be the best customer service."

"But it was a good night numbers wise?"

"Great," Kelly said.

I thought about that fiasco for about three minutes, then I went to bed. But I tossed and turned and tried to calm my racing mind and hormones to no avail. At some point I checked the time with one eye open hoping it would have said 6, but it didn't; it said 3:10. Arggh.

Rousing myself from the bed that would offer no sleep, I sat on the edge thinking. It might be a good time to get into room 237—I still had the key. The desk in the lobby would be manned, but at that hour whoever was there might be snoozing.

I threw some clothes on just in case I was apprehended, and rooted around in one of the gift bags looking for the mini *What About Bob?* flashlight. Voila. I tried it to see if it actually worked, and it did. It would have been perfect if I were looking for a speck in my eye. Alas, it would take me a month to illuminate every inch of that room. And an inch is about as much as that light made visible. You use the tools you have.

No shoes. That might be a good idea, I thought, so I quietly opened the door to room 239, left it ajar, and tiptoed barefoot down the corridor. I peeped around the wall to check if I could see anybody at the front desk before I made a beeline for room 237. There was not a sound to be heard except my heart beating like the bass in one of Neil's favorite bands, Echo and The Bunnymen: boom ba boom ba boom. Like that.

I slipped the key into the lock, opened the door to a dark room except for a pale grey light coming from the window. Switching on the tiny blue flashlight, I found the chalk outline had been removed. It was hard to see if the blood had been cleaned completely, but my guess was that sooner or later that carpet was going to be replaced. It was way too dark for me to look for a bug in the room. That would have to wait for daylight. Pussyfooting across the carpet in front of the window I stepped on something sharp that stuck in my foot. When I shined the light on it as I sat on the bed, I found what looked like a dried up contact lens. A distant bell struck in my brain, but I wasn't sure why. I plucked the contact from my foot, stuck it into my pocket, and shined the light on the walls. I swept the light in an arc revealing a cheesy horse painting, a broken sconce, and the connecting door to the next room. Then I had an epiphany.

A body could have been moved through those connecting doors. If someone had the wherewithal they could unlock all the doors—from 237 to 249—then move a body into the outside hall with access to the back stairs and back door.

As much as I missed the sex with Neil that night, and I did miss it, I might not have figured this out, or found the contact lens—if that was an actual clue. Poor Neil. I was a real dick. But I really wanted to be a Private Dick.

Unlatching the connecting door from room 237, I figured I'd do a better search for a bug and whatever else I might find the next day. I exited the door, crept down the corridor as quietly as I could, and pushed open my door. Curiously it seemed more ajar than I had left it. Probably the hotel shifting with age I thought before I caught sight of a dark figure quickly hunching beside the bed next to the window. My heart started pumping again like that damn bass, but I slipped slowly across the carpet, and picked up the first thing that I saw that had any heft—the Glade Country Pottery diffuser. I lunged across the bed and whacked the intruder with all the might I had in my right arm. They jumped up with surprising agility given the small space, and sprinted out the door. It took me a second to rally, but once I did, I darted after them. Then nothing. They were gone. I looked up, down, everywhere. Was it Spiderman?

The thought occurred to me to go to the pool, retrieve Neil, and have him stay with me. But then I thought better of it. I called down to the desk to tell them somebody had entered my room. I didn't, of course, tell them that I had left the door open while I was poking around in the room next door. I asked them to summon the police, even though, in the back of my mind, I thought this meant more time for me in Wonderly. But who was that? What did they want? Was it a man or a woman? I wanted my Moms!

I sat terrorized at the edge of the bed willing myself to put all the pieces together. And although there were lots of pieces, none of them fit. At that moment the most perplexing jigsaw piece was whether the person in my room was there because I was peeping around next door or for some other reason? But what could that be?

Two policemen arrived about fifteen minutes later. They called my room to ask me to meet them in the lobby, which I did. I told them a slightly different version of the truth, so I'd better tell you, too.

"I was asleep in my bed, officer. I heard a slight rustling, I think, that woke me. It startled me to realize somebody was crouching beside the bed by the window. I blindly reached for something to protect myself. When I felt the person move, I hit them over the head with a Glade Country Pottery

Diffuser that I had bought to cover the smell of cigarette smoke left by hundreds of prior guests."

Way too much information. I could tell by the bored looks on their faces.

They said they'd like to go up to the room to examine it. Thank goodness I hadn't yet unlocked my side of the door connecting room 237.

An examination of the room by officers Hines and Duncan apparently uncovered no evidence that could name the intruder. A crime scene unit appeared to dust the room for fingerprints shortly after the officers had finished looking around.

"Oh, officer. I did have a visitor from my store in Ohio; so you may find his fingerprints."

"Are they still in town? We'll need to have the fingerprints to eliminate them," Officer Hines instructed.

"He's leaving tomorrow. Can you get the prints in the morning?" I asked.

"Shouldn't be a problem. We can get yours then, too," Hines answered.

When the door closed on the police and the crime scene unit, the clock said four thirteen. I had nothing to do that day but bid Neil good-bye and go to a party at Dun Wonderly's. So I could sleep all day. Then again I needed to get my fingerprints taken with Neil, I sure hoped I could meet with Chief Earl, and I sure hoped that would be later in the day so I could rest.

It seemed like I'd just laid my head on the pillow when I heard a key in the door. That got me to my feet pronto. The only thing on the night table now was the tiny *What About Bob?* flashlight, and I grabbed it. What was I going to do with that? Shine a pinprick of light up their nose?

"Oh, good. You're up," said Neil, looking like he'd had as little sleep as I had.

"You have to have your fingerprints taken," I said rubbing the sleep out of my eyes.

"What did *I* do?" he puzzled.

"Somebody broke into my room last night. I clocked them over the head with my diffuser, but they got away. Besides mine, the cleaning woman's—and maybe the intruder's— yours are the only other fingerprints that might be here. Oh, except for anybody else who's ever been in this room. So before you leave, we have to go to the police station and stick our fingers on that black stuff to compare ours to the bad guy ... or gal." But, really, can a would-be killer be called a gal?

"Crikey, I'm in the middle of a who-dunnit," Neil boasted.

"I'm up now, but I didn't get a lick of sleep. Did you sleep?" I asked.

"Hardly. Why is it so easy to fall asleep in the sun on one of those lounges, but impossible when it's dark? And there were swimmers, or a swimmer, and somebody else who was yelling."

"Did you see who they were?" I asked.

"Hell no. If I even moved on that flimsy thing I was bound to fall over, and the way it's going around here, I could be dead by now."

"What did you hear?"

"I think I might have fallen asleep with the blanket over my head when I woke up hearing a splash in the pool. I didn't think anything of it, but I could hear someone swimming for what seemed like ten minutes or so. Then I heard a door open and footsteps. Then just the splashing of the person swimming."

"And then what?" I urged.

"Then I heard two people talking. I couldn't tell if they were men or women or a man and a woman, but they were yelling at each other. It sounded like we were in an echo chamber."

"Then what?" I pushed.

"Then one of them said 'What are you, the bottom or the top? Or you like both?'"

"Geez, that was getting pretty personal, if they were talking about sex," I said, stating the obvious.

"Then one of them started screaming, 'You miserable twat monger, I'm giving you fair warning, back off'."

"That was definitely a threat, but you couldn't tell if it was a man or a woman?"

"I couldn't, but it stopped when someone came out of one of the rooms around the pool and said, 'Hey keep it down, we're trying to sleep.' Then I only heard whispering, then more footsteps, and finally the door to the pool slammed, so I guess the one not in the pool left. There was nobody floating in the pool or at the bottom when I left this morning, so that was the end of it."

If there was a bug in the room, they'd pick up on Neil's poolside escapade; I had to do a serious search in at least 239 for a bug. A bug in 237 might tell me who killed Bobby Crane ... far more important.

CHAPTER 14

I took a shower first, being careful to use only one of the flimsy towels so Neil had a dry one to use for himself. He uses about ten paper towels in the store to dry his hands after washing them—towels *I* pay for. He wasn't going to like only one towel for his whole body, but he had no choice. Knowing him as I now do, I've come to learn he fits the description "champagne taste, beer pocketbook" to a tee. When we dine out together, he likes the chic places, the expensive dishes on the menu, the best wine, the fanciest desserts. I can't say it's not fun, but he must live like a pauper the rest of the time to save up for those gala events he insists on paying for. Or he's a trust fund kid. I doubt that though.

Even freshly showered and dried, both in black jeans and black T-shirts, we still looked like a couple of basset hounds with enough bags under our eyes to take an around-the-world tour. As we sluggishly walked to Neil's car for our fingerprinting excursion, I felt a sense of guilt. That teensy lie I told the police the night before was nagging at me.

It was nine thirty-five and it felt like half the day was gone already. I wished it was. I was bone-deep tired like when Bogie was an infant with colic, or Iggy was screeching through the night with one of her earaches. My poor babies, but Mama was pooped back then and now again.

The Wonderly police department was on Placid Drive off of Pleasant Street. They were really trying to sell a laid-back vibe for this town. The red brick Cape Cod police building could have housed a happy family, but it didn't. It was the domicile of the town's peace keepers.

"I sure didn't think I'd be fingerprinted while I was supposed to be visiting Hollywood in Kentucky," Neil said as we made our way up the cobblestone walk.

"Life's full of fun surprises," I bantered.

Neil held the door for me as we entered a small lobby where a woman whose name tag said Amanda was seated at a desk. "Howdy, how can I help you?"

"We're here to have our fingerprints taken. There was a break-in of my room at The Dunbar Hotel last night . . . well, really this morning," I corrected myself

"Honey, you don't have to tell me the story. I just answer the phones. I'll let someone know you're here," she muttered, pushing a button on the black desk phone. All she said when someone picked up was "Fingerprints."

"They'll be right out. Have a seat," she instructed.

Our fannies hadn't even hit the seats when a cop came out, "Fingerprints?" he asked, looking our way.

"Yep," Neil answered.

"Come on in," he instructed.

We followed the hefty fingerprint guy through a heavy white door to offices down the hall. The place was spotless. Either they didn't have many crimes and spent their time cleaning, or they had great janitor.

We told Officer Roberts why we were there. "Hah, good luck finding out who might have been in there aside from you," he said looking us up and down. I was familiar with this look of judgment from small-minded people who frowned upon age differences. What did they know? Matchy matchy isn't always great.

"How many people do you think left their fingerprints in that room besides you?"

"We're here because the detectives asked us to have our prints taken," I explained.

"Okay, for whatever good it will do," he demurred, shaking his bulldog head. He had a prominent scar from the corner of his lip to his ear, and I wondered if a bullet had seared his cheek. In Wonderly?

Neil went first, and I could tell from his body language he was pretty pleased with himself. Fingerprinting always seemed kind of cool as if you were Nicholas Cage in *Raising Arizona*. But as I pressed my fingertips into the black soot I felt guilt, not pleasure. I didn't do anything wrong, but how on earth did I get myself into the middle of another murder case? I chalked it up to inferior timing.

As I was pondering my fate, Amanda stuck her head in the door. "Miss Fillmore, Chief Earl would like to see you."

"Will it be long?" I asked. "My friend drove me from the hotel, and he has to go back to Cincinnati this morning."

"Hold on," Amanda requested.

Neil and I looked at each other while we were wiping the black powder from our fingers. His gaze had a hint of sorrow, and I felt the same way about his leaving.

"Chief says someone will drive you back to the hotel," Amanda said, sticking her head around the door.

"Okay. I'll just walk my friend to his car to say good-bye."

"He wants to see you now," she kind of demanded.

I paid no attention to her though, but opened the door, and we walked to Neil's car. We hugged good-bye and he got into his car. I don't know what came over me, but I reached through his open window, grabbed his swarthy, sturdy neck and kissed him more passionately than might have been appropriate for a Sunday morning.

"Cripes, nothing like two thousand pounds of steel between us to get you aroused," he joked.

"Leftovers from last night, I guess."

"Should I stay?" he asked

"No. You should go. But thank you for coming down. It was good to have you here in wonderful Wonderly."

"Wonderland's a weird name for a place with all these murders," he declared.

"It's Wonder-lee," I articulated.

"Whatever. Later," he said as he backed out. I watched him and his white Volkswagen with regret as he took off down Placid Street.

Amanda didn't say a word when I re-entered the building. Her disapproval was palpable.

She led me down another grey-tweed-carpeted hall, adorned with photos of previous chiefs. When we got to the end, she knocked on a door at the right. We heard a buzz, then she opened the door announcing, "Here she is."

"Mrs. Fillmore, please come in," Chief Earl said.

"Ms. Fillmore," I corrected him.

"Welcome to Wonderly," he greeted me.

"It would have been better if Jessica wasn't dead," I answered.

"You know Jessica, I've been told," he said, leaning forward on his desk—his spotless desk—elbows on the shiny surface, chin resting on his hands. His hazel eyes narrowed under unruly white brows.

"I met her, but I don't, didn't, know her. I was having dinner at The Wonder on Friday night, and she was in the bar crying, and I asked her to join me. She was the girl who checked me in Friday morning and gave me the wrong key. Have you heard about that?" I asked.

"It's always good to hear everybody's version," he said dryly urging me to go on.

"Well, she gave me the key to room two thirty-seven, and when I entered, I saw a chalk outline of what I assumed had been a dead body. The body was gone, but a large amount of dried blood was still there.

"When I called down to see if it was a joke, Mr. Wonderly and a few others, including Jessica, came up to tell me it wasn't what it looked like. It was kind of a joke, I think Mr. Wonderly said."

"And did Jessica say it was a joke?" he asked leaning even closer to me over his desk.

"No. Jessica didn't say anything. She did sit on the steps and cry after Mr. Wonderly fired her," I told him.

"Do you know any of the other reps or desk clerks at Wonderly?" he pressed.

"I only know my inside rep and my outside rep. Well, I just met Linda, my inside rep, since I've been here. Rob Woodbury calls on me at my store in Briartown, which is north of Cincinnati."

"And you haven't met anybody else here in Wonderly?"

Um.

"Just the local shopkeepers on Pleasant Street. That's all I can recall. Oh, and Dun Wonderly and his sidekick, Bucky."

"Sidekick?"

"Maybe assistant is a better word. I'm not sure exactly what his title is," I fumbled.

I couldn't mention Alice Bostick. I just couldn't betray her trust. And how would he know if I'd seen her unless he knew one of the mourners who saw me coming out of Alice's house yesterday. Yesterday? It seemed like I'd been in Wonderly for a month already.

"And what were you doing between ten-thirty and midnight Friday night?" he asked.

"I got back to my room after dinner and I needed scissors, so I went down to the lobby. The clock said ten forty-five, and as I was walking down the stairs I saw who I think might have been Jessica running under the staircase back toward the warehouse. I mean I don't know if it was Jessica, and I don't know if whoever it was, was heading toward the warehouse, but that's what I thought at the time," I said.

"Why?" he asked me, not moving his head but raising his bushy eyebrows.

"Why what?" I asked.

"Why did you think it might have been Jessica?"

"Because the last time I saw her she had been wearing a jean jacket that looked like the jacket the girl with the curly blond hair who was running toward the warehouse was wearing. And Jessica had curly blond hair."

"Okay. Did you see anybody else in the lobby?"

"Just Rachel. The girl at the registration desk."

"Do you know Ty Patton?" he asked, still with the raised eyebrows.

"I don't know him, but I've heard from a few of the reps that he was the warehouse manager and Jessica's boyfriend."

I could have told him that Ty and Jessica were having an argument at The Wonder bar, but I didn't. The bartender could tell him that if he were interviewed.

"Mrs. Fillmore, most of the attendees at the convention are going home Tuesday. You and a few others will have to hang around, since it seems you have—wittingly or unwittingly—inserted yourself into this case.

"It's Ms. Fillmore. And, Inserted? How have I inserted myself? I just spoke with Jessica at dinner, that's all."

"Actually, you were the last person to speak with her as far as we know," he said sitting back in his seat and widening his eyes.

"Well, I clearly wasn't the last person. The last person would be the person who killed her," I said with more snark in my voice than I should have used.

"So you think she was murdered and it wasn't an accident?" Emphasis on *you*.

"How would I know for sure? I thought that's what you said." I parried.

"No, I didn't say that," he said, crossing his arms and sitting back from his desk.

"Oh, sorry," I said. "And what about the dead body in room two thirty-seven. I didn't actually see a dead body, but I did see chalk outlining what looked like a body and a lot of dried blood in the middle of that chalked outline. What about him?"

He just stared at me.

I stared back.

"Don't leave town, Mrs. Fillmore, until I personally say you can leave. Is that clear?"

Crystal was my first thought, but I kept that to myself. "Yes sir," I replied instead. And, I didn't mention *again* that it was Ms. and not Mrs. He wasn't going to call me Ms... ever.

"I'll have an officer drive you back to your hotel," the chief said, rising from his chair indicating to me I should get lost.

Fatigue overtook me in the short drive from the police station to the hotel, and Officer Cruz kept looking over at me as my head bobbled forward and backward. "You okay?" he asked.

"Just tired and hungry. I need to sleep the rest of the day. Any chance we can stop for donuts and coffee? It's on me," I suggested. And so we did.

CHAPTER 15

My wish to sleep the afternoon away was short-lived because who do you think was sitting in one of the rococo chairs in the lobby as I entered? Yep, Marilyn Monroe, my friend, not the dead Hollywood star.

"Surprise," she said as she saw me.

"Wow, I must really be missed!" I exclaimed.

"Well, that and I had to get away from the house that's lousy with people. It's amazing how one small baby can make an ordinary house seem like a Jim Jones cocktail party. It was either come down here for a day or homicide."

"I'm glad you're here, but I *have* to sleep. Now," I kind of begged. I explained what had happened, purposely omitting the kissing with Neil. "But let me fill you in on what's been happening while we go to my room. We'll take the elevator…I'm way too pooped to walk another step. So I told her. Everything.

"You slept with him, didn't you? Good for you."

"I did not sleep with him. For God's sake."

"Okay, okay. The lady doth protest too much if you ask me, but if you say you didn't…You know what? You sleep. I'll take a walk downtown. There is a downtown isn't there?" she asked.

"Not exactly Manhattan, but it might just be your speed. It has some nice little stores and a great little restaurant, The Wonder. Also, I hear there's a barbeque place that makes Wonderly a destination of sorts. But we're invited to Mr. Wonderly's house tonight for a soirée. And if his house is anything like his office, wear a tiara."

"Seriously? I have nothing appropriate to wear. What are you wearing?"

"What do I usually wear?"

"Black?"

"Yes. I brought accessories to go with my black dress, but they're beginning to wear out their novelty. If you see something tantalizing to go with black, pick me up a new necklace and earrings while you're shopping for a satin dress."

"I don't really have to buy a satin dress, do I?" she asked looking forlorn.

"Of course not. Being here for almost a full three days is causing me to break out in hyperbole. I need the excitement."

"You don't think two dead people are exciting enough?" she asked.

"I'm not sure I would call that exciting— more like horrifying."

"Right," she said as we were finally to my room.

Exhaustion overtook me as I walked into the room, and I was asleep as soon as I hit the bed. Regrettably, not a restful sleep—but one of those herky-jerky afternoon naps. This one had me dreaming of making love to Neil on a rickety vinyl lounge chair. The distressing part was every time we were about to seal the deal, the flimsy strapped chair would dump us on the floor.

A rap on the door made me jump, knocking over the damn lounge chair for the last time. "Yes?" I croaked from my sweaty bed.

"It's me, Marilyn."

Stumbling like Chevy Chase in an SNL skit, I managed to blurt out, "I'm coming. "I'm coming."

There she stood with a shopping bag, looking like she'd just run a marathon, "One word. Mutton," she said.

"Mutton? What does that mean?"

"That barbeque place you told me about, The Butt Hut? There was a buffet with all kinds of meat including mutton. Who eats mutton? I thought that was a joke meat."

"Apparently not a joke in Wonderly. Did you try it?"

"Are you kidding? I didn't try anything. Anything made in the same kitchen as mutton wouldn't be anything I'd eat. I stopped and got some candy at a place called Delilah's, and ate that while I was walking back here."

"How were your other shopping adventures?"

"I had to buy a used dress. Finery Boutique, the only store with new dresses, was too finery for my pocketbook. Must be money in these here parts because three hundred fifty dollars for a plain dress is out of my range. So I went to the Antique Mall, and they had some okay used dresses. I hope you don't gag when you see what I bought," she pleaded.

"Let's see," I said, grabbing the bag out of her hand.

"No, let me try it on so you can get the full picture," she said, grabbing it back, and headed for the bathroom.

In truth Marilyn would look good in anything. At five foot nine she was lithe and willowy. I never did see her take advantage of her assets, but she could have easily been a model.

She emerged a few minutes later in a red-and-white polka dot swing-skirted dress with a red rolled collar. My first thought was a young and beautiful Cousin Minnie Pearl. Because of her height, the skirt was shorter on her than the original owner, I'm guessing, but it showcased her legs—which I'm not sure I'd ever seen before.

"Well, zowie. Why don't you wear dresses more often?" I asked.

"You don't think three boys are enough?" she joked.

"What are you going to wear on your feet?"

"Sneakers. That's all I have. They're white, so they'll go with the dots," she answered.

"And you'll be at the ready when the square dancing begins."

"Will there be square dancing?" she asked in all earnestness.

"Just pulling your chain. But you'll out-dazzle them even in your white sneakers. Did you manage to find a necklace and earrings for me?"

"It wasn't easy, unless you wanted to spend a few hundred bucks or wear a horseshoe around your neck. There's a lot of horse stuff down here. I bought this at the antique mall where I bought my dress."

She pulled a small packet out of her shopping bag and unfolded it to reveal my new old necklace. It was a white cameo pendant, with red and white stones nestled in filigree hanging from a mottled gold chain. The earrings were the same but smaller. Well, I'd stand out, and a bargain at eight dollars for both.

"Perfect," I told her.

"Do you really like them? They're kind of ugly, but the only necklace and earring set I could find."

Changing the subject, I said, "Let's watch the Bare Bottom Babes video. You know, the one I told you about that Dun Wonderly produced? I want to see if I can spot anything that might hint at what happened to Jessica—and maybe the dead guy, Bobby Crane."

She curled her lip, "Yuck, but if you think it'll help."

We pulled the two chairs from the table in front of the window up to the TV, and I slipped the BBB video into the VCR mouth. The customary black-and-white static gave way to glorious aquamarine waters lapping on white sand. The Beach Boys' *Kokomo* provided the sound track.

As we sat there drooling at the location, a young woman in a yellow thong bikini emerged as the BARE BOTTOM BABES logo appeared on the screen. The camera had cut off her head just like the standee at the convention. But, honestly, nobody would be looking at her from the neck up anyway. She jogged into the water in slow motion, highlighting her perfectly round, non-dimpled rump.

"Come on," observed Marilyn, "nobody's ass looks like that."

"I think you're wrong. Women spend a lot of time getting their behinds to look like that. There are probably a lot more, so hang on," I warned.

The next half hour was spent by Marilyn *omygodding* as we watched a bevy of backsides cavorting in the water, bending over, bending sideways, occasionally patting themselves on their posteriors, and so much more. Whoever directed this little photoplay must have been dreaming it up for a long time. I had no idea bottoms could be so versatile.

Every behind was a thing of beauty: some sleek, some bouncy, and one particularly bounteous in its perfection and size as it billowed out from the tiniest of waists, a black thong barely visible.

"I mean, seriously, have you ever seen a can like that before? It can't be real," Marilyn marveled.

I wondered if Marilyn, like me, was thinking of jogging up and down our steps to reach even a modicum of that kind of perfection in the back.

"All they must do is work out to get their asses looking like that. What a waste of time," she said, putting to rest my thought that she might have been sharing my fantasy.

Was that the same bounteous bottom as the decapitated BBB booth standee? It could have been; none of the others on the beach seemed quite so fulsome.

"Did I tell you about the giant standee at the Bare Bottom Babe booth on the convention floor?"

"Yeah. The one who was decapitated?" she answered.

"Right the cardboard slashing. It had to be cut off because a bit of face was recognizable, don't you think?"

"Who needs a face when you have a butt as recognizable as any of these, even covered with clothes?"

The more that thought rolled around in my brain, the more I think I was right—maybe the really curvy girl's booty was the same one on the standee.

"How about we shower, get dressed, and have a drink at the bar before we go to the Wonderly fête this evening?

"Sounds good. Do you want to go first?" Marilyn asked.

"No, you go, but easy on the towels. They're thin and not many of them."

"Gotcha," she said gathering up her toiletries and heading for the bathroom.

I thought about catching a few more winks, but then the adjoining door to the neighboring room caught my eye.

I tiptoed across the carpet and turned the sturdy brass lock to room 237. Why was I tiptoeing barefooted? Guilt—I knew I shouldn't have been going in there.

A sliver of light from between the curtains lay across an upturned table. Once fully in the room I saw all the furniture was on its side or upside down. And, those curtains were opened the last time I was in this room. Weren't they? The mattress was unencumbered by sheets, covers, and spread. Did the police do this last night? Or did somebody else? I thought I'd never find out, but when I tripped over a pink flashlight by the bed, it was evident it wasn't a police job.

Somebody was looking for something, but what, the bug? Or could it be the contact lens I found now hiding in my make-up case? Looking around the room for likely places to hide a bug, the only place that I lit on was the smoke detector. I'd have to check that out.

"What's going on?" called Marilyn.

Making a hasty retreat back to my room, I found Marilyn standing by the window in all her hoedown glory. She looked beautiful, but definitely like she was heading out to a barn dance.

"Too bad it's not a costume party," she said. "Can I really wear this?"

"Your beauty will out-dazzle your dress. Seriously," I consoled.

"What were you doing next door?" Marilyn inquired.

"Take a look at this mess," I said, pointing into room 237. "Somebody's been here looking for something."

"You don't have what they're looking for I hope. I don't want you ending up dead in Wonderly," she said.

"No. We don't want that. But I'm getting dressed. I'll think about that later," I lied.

Once I showered and put on my black dress with the cameo necklace and earrings, I looked like I was going to a funeral. A fine pair we made, but who cared? Nobody knew us. Not yet.

CHAPTER 16

A bustling bar greeted us as we made our way through the crush of people. "Bar seat okay for you?" I asked.

"Heck, yes. Better actually," Marilyn responded, and nudged me toward two empty stools. "I get out so little, the more people the better for me. It makes me feel like I'm actually alive."

After about ten minutes of no attendance, Marilyn leaned over the bar, pushing up her cleavage. "How does someone get a drink around here," she bellowed down the bar toward the guy flipping bottles like Tom Cruise in *Cocktail.*

"Just ask," a bartender said, squeezing his way behind other bodies behind the bar. "What can I get for you two out-of-towners," he asked.

"A beer for me, draft, and a white wine for my girlfriend. Or do you want Scotch?" Marilyn asked.

"White wine is good," I answered. "The only thing I've eaten today is three glazed donuts and two cups of coffee. So no Scotch until I get food in me."

"Even with the square-dance dress he thinks we're out-of-towners. What do you have to wear to look like a local?" she asked.

"For starters," said the male drawl behind us, "I'd do tweed."

"Andy Wonderly," he said holding out his hand to Marilyn and then to me. In fact he was looking quite tweedy in blue jeans like he was wearing the night before, a wool jacket, and blue button down.

We shook hands.

This guy looked so much unlike his brother they could have been from different galaxies: tall, broad shoulders, flat stomach, smelling like a cologne advertisement in GQ. His grey eyes were taking in every inch of Marilyn. I could see her squirming.

"My you smell wonderful," I said in an attempt to divert his gaze away from her.

"Chanel Égoïste," he answered

You didn't have to be from France to know what that means. His egotisim reeked.

"What brings you lovely ladies to Wonderly?" he inquired of Marilyn.

"I attended the video convention, but now I have to stay a few more days," I butted in.

"Ah do hope you're going to be at Dun's this evening? Please say you are?" he gushed.

"As a matter of fact, we are," I responded. Marilyn seemed to have gone mute.

"I insist on paying for your drinks and driving you over. That way you don't have to squeeze into a limo with the others." He made it sound as if "the others" might have the bubonic plague.

"How very kind," I said. What's wrong with me? Can't I talk with these people without sounding like I just came off the set of *Gone With the Wind*?

We each had another drink, Andy drinking Maker's Mark out of a cut crystal tumbler. I didn't notice other glasses at the bar were cut crystal. No doubt he received special attention because he was a Wonderly. I had to pinch myself to not ask him for a sip. I wasn't a bourbon drinker, but I was pretty sure whatever was in that fancy glass would be mighty tasty.

"My car's right out front, so you won't have to walk far," Andy pointed out as we were getting ready to leave.

Good lord, if this was the Corvette he was driving the night before, he was going to have to throw me in the trunk.

But it wasn't, it was a long black Cadillac. Andy steered Marilyn to the front seat by her elbow, and she went along nicely. She must have been in shock, because she's not one to be steered that I've ever noticed. He did open the back door for me which was a nice touch since I'm pretty sure he thought of me as extra baggage.

The cream-colored leather seats made me feel as if I was being held in the palm of a French calfskin glove. It reminded me of the pair of cream-colored gloves Uncle Fred gave me for my thirteenth birthday. I slept with them on for the first three nights until Helen told me I was going to stretch them and they wouldn't look as lovely as I wanted for my first dance.

I was in a creamy leather daze when Marilyn finally spoke. "I'm going home tomorrow morning. My husband and five boys need me."

"*Five* boys?" Andy issued loudly.

She must have given birth to two of them after we left the bar.

Of course, I knew Marilyn well enough to know that she exaggerates when she wants to make a point. I believe her point might have been well taken, because Andy asked over his shoulder, "You married, Annie?"

Taking a cue from Marilyn, I answered, "Yep."

"Here we are," Andy informed us as we drove around a circular drive to what looked like a castle in Disneyland. Lights were blazing in every room, a three-tiered fountain burbled in the center of the lawn around which the drive curved. Dun Wonderly stood at the portico beside two massive doors that were open to a wide hallway.

"Geez," Marilyn murmured.

"Yep, he's rich, but without an ounce of good taste," commented Andy.

He let us out of the Caddy, and bounced out of the car himself as a teenage boy took the wheel and drove it somewhere out of sight.

"Wail, Annie Fillmore. So glad you could make it. Ah see you came with my brother. Wail," Dun said, not looking at Andy who seemed pretty blasé about being snubbed.

"May I introduce my associate, Marilyn Monroe? She's staying with me tonight," I explained, so unnecessarily.

"Ah have to say the real Marilyn Monroe has nothing on you," he offered unabashedly, stepping back a bit to look her up and down.

"Go on in an' meet ma wife, Sugar, and the other guests," he prompted.

As we entered the hallway, all I could see was marble, gold, and masses of purple orchids. This was over-over-the-top. A woman with blond hair swooped into an elaborate up do complemented the ornate furniture. She was wearing a pink satin flowing caftan with lace insets at the shoulders and down the arms. I assumed that was Sugar. She didn't look like she was about to be dumped, as Jessica had told me. But how would I know how people who lived like this acted?

I whispered to Marilyn that I thought the woman in pink was Dun's wife and we should meet her and thank her for her hospitality. More importantly, I wanted to find out what manner of woman would be married to the likes of Dun Wonderly. When we were waiting to meet her, I could smell the perfume, "Poison," a scent that immediately gives me a headache and makes my stomach churn. As we got closer, the aroma acted like a barrier, shielding Sugar from anybody getting too close. Maybe that was the point.

"Welcome to our home," Sugar drawled in a raspy voice with a suggestion of cigarettes and booze. But who could blame her for any escape she had to take to ease her pain for her marital mistake.

"Thank you so much, Mrs. Wonderly, for your hospitality. I'm Annie Fillmore, a customer of Wonderly Entertainment, and this is my associate, Marilyn Monroe."

She turned to an elaborate gold-colored wood console table topped with matching mirror, picked up a heavy glass, and downed the amber liquid in one gulp. She looked at Marilyn, threw her head back and barked a tough old broad laugh, "Now why the hell didn't I think of calling myself Marilyn Monroe. That's just splendid."

She won me over with one laugh.

Marilyn explained how she came to have the same name as the bounteous Marilyn, and Mrs. Wonderly yelped, "That's your story and you should stick with it. And for Lawd's sake call me Sugar. I feel like your elderly aunt otherwise. Come on girls, I'll take you for a tour of this dump." Then another wonderful belly laugh.

We followed Sugar into a solarium that opened off the living room, and, surprisingly, it had no gold embellishment. White sofas and deep cushioned white chairs set on jute rugs. Now this was a room I could call home.

"This is my room," she croaked. "The only one I was allowed to decorate. That was after Dun got so rich that when he bought a new boat he'd get a new one when the first one got wet," she said, barking out another guffaw. "He bought this house and transplanted us from our perfect Cape Cod downtown. Luckily, Jamie and Debbie were graduating high school so they didn't have to know the profound sadness of leaving their home to rattle around in this gold Easter egg monstrosity.

"This *is* a lovely room," I agreed. Marilyn had sunk into one of the white chairs and was looking like she wouldn't move.

"Are Debbie and Jamie twins," asked Marilyn.

"Perfect twins. After they graduated from high school they went to California, got their undergraduate degrees at Pepperdine, then on to UC Berkeley for their Masters. Dun practically had a hissy fit at them going to such a liberal institution, but they prevailed. Bless 'em. I love it 'cause I get to visit them and enjoy that perfect weather. I might just join them out there if we can ever get around this can of worms," she exhaled, bringing her empty glass toward her lips again.

"Can of worms?" I questioned.

"Well, you're not from here, so you might not know what the whole damn town knows, but that ole Dun thinks is a secret. He's been playing hanky-panky with a waitress over at the The Butt Hut. I think she's about twenty-two. He's sixty-seven. She must like gold," Sugar confided.

The Butt Hut? That place must have been named by the same person who named Boo-Kay Florist.

Marilyn and I looked at each other, waiting for one of us to speak. Marilyn went first, "How terrible for you, Sugar."

"It's not the fling that bothers me. He's been flinging his thing around since we were married. It's that he thinks I'm stupid enough not to know. Don't piss on my leg and tell me it's rainin'. He's done that for years, and I'm fed up and ready for him to move on, the constipated old fart. But I get the jitters that he won't move on, that he thinks this arrangement is fine and dandy. Then I might have to murder him," she said, coughing over her growling laugh.

"I sure hope it works out for you, Sugar," I said.

"Hell, me too, but right now my eyeballs are floatin', I'll catch you later," she said as she skimmed across the marble floor.

"Let's get some grub and a drink," Marilyn urged.

The house was crowded as we made our way to the dining room, where a line was circling a massive oval table laid with a lavish buffet. A young woman in a French maid costume proffered a gilded tray of champagne glasses with strawberries nestled in the bubbles. Marilyn plucked one up for her, then held the girl's arm to get another for me.

As I was about to ask Marilyn what she thought of our interlude with Sugar, a tap on my shoulder stopped me mid-thought. "Good evening," said Bucky Henderson. I knew by now he wouldn't remember my name, so I helped him out by introducing myself to his wife. "Hi, Mrs. Henderson, I'm Annie Fillmore and this is my friend, Marilyn Monroe."

"Hey, you're famous," said Bucky to Marilyn.

What a doofus.

Vivian Henderson, as she introduced herself, said to Marilyn, "Great name. Married name?"

"Yes, my married name. My mother wouldn't have done that to me," responded Marilyn.

Adjusting his heavy black-rimmed eyeglasses, Bucky asked, "Are you ladies enjoying this magnificent home?"

"Very nice," answered Marilyn.

"Bucky, stop fiddling," urged Vivian.

A closer look at Vivian made me think she should have been on a Paris runway modelling the latest Dior instead of mingling here in Wonderland. Her red hair was cut in a sleek glossy bob with eye-grazing bangs. Maybe there was a small pool of men to choose from when Vivian decided to marry. Her cream and black polka dot silk dress was too posh for even the high-end retail shop in Wonderly. This was designer. Checking out Bucky close up and personal made me realize he was kind of handsome in an "oh gosh ma'am" sort of way. Maybe that's what drew her to him, or he could be rich…that can turn a lot of women's heads. Sadly, it never has turned mine.

As we walked away from the Hendersons, I turned to Marilyn, and I asked, "What do you think of Bucky?"

"Cute, don't you think?" she responded.

"Kind of goofy, don't *you* think?" I parried.

"Okay, cute and goofy," she agreed.

Obviously, we were filling time until we made it to the table, where a roasted pig lay complete with an apple in its mouth.

A rumble from behind turned our heads. Dun Wonderly was making his way through the guests like Moses parting the Red Sea.

"Everybody havin' a good time? Enjoying the food? Heh heh heh. Ol Dun is havin' the tahm of his life."

Why do some people refer to themselves in the third person? Caesar and Nixon did it. I guess Dun Wonderly held himself in the same high esteem.

"I wonder what happened to Sugar?" I asked Marilyn rhetorically. "It would be interesting to see them interacting, don't you think?"

"Why? That poor woman's put up with him all these years. If she's hiding in the butler's pantry drinking, good on her."

That thought was interrupted by Daisy Dixon, "You have another guest?" she asked smiling at Marilyn.

"Yes, this is my friend who also works at my store, Marilyn Monroe." I just waited.

"Is Marilyn Monroe your sister or something," Daisy inquired.

You can't make this stuff up.

"No. Monroe is my married name," she answered for what must have been at least the thousandth time since she and Tom married.

Since Marilyn was engaged in conversation—whether she wanted to be or not—I took the opportunity to look around the house. I wasn't looking for decorating tips, that's for sure.

CHAPTER 17

A couple of right turns found me in the kitchen, where there were three people refilling gold and silver trays.

"Hi," I said.

"Do you need something?" one of the servers asked.

" I'm looking for the ladies room," I prevaricated with the first thing that came to my lips.

"There's one in the back through the kitchen that we use, or one in the foyer where you came in. I hear there are five more someplace, maybe upstairs."

That was an invitation, wasn't it? Go upstairs to find one of the five bathrooms. I'm sure it was. "

"Thanks," I said, wandering back to the front door and the imposing staircase that I hoped was going to take me to a clue. Any clue.

Fortunately, there was no one in the foyer to notice me nosing around. Despite its tacky gold handrail, the spiral staircase enticed me up the steps.

Halfway up I encountered Sugar descending. "Need something, honey?" she asked.

"I'm looking for a ladies room."

"Hmm. Your rep, Linda, just told me all about you and the crime that happened in your stomping ground last year and how you helped the police solve the murder."

"Well," I stammered.

"If you're looking for something juicy, third floor, fourth door on your left," she said with a wink.

That was more of a direction than a suggestion, so up I went. The second floor was carpeted in lush cream, and the peach walls were hung with old family photographs. Were these really the faces of Wonderly forefathers? Maybe. Or perhaps someone got a good deal at Wittler's Antique Mall.

At the end of the elegant hall were a set of plain wooden stairs, like an "Upstairs Downstairs" vibe.

I climbed to the carpetless third floor, where the white walls were unadorned by ancestors. It was a long hallway, and I counted four doors down. I listened at the door first, and I heard some low music, so I knocked.

"Is that you, my honey pie?" I heard a young woman's husky voice call out.

Where I got the hutzpah to open the door and enter I don't know. But I did. And there stood a shapely girl in a French maid costume bent over without any underwear. If that wasn't enough of a jolt, the long chain around her ankle shackling her to the black wrought iron bed frame underscored the shock. This scene made Bare Bottom Babes seem PG-13.

She turned around when she heard me, looking stunned, "Who the hell are you?"

"Let me unhook you from the bed. Oh, my God, how did you get like this? I'll get you out of here," I said as soothingly as I could muster.

"Get me out of here? Why? Dun will be up in about a minute, and he'll want me just like this," she huffed.

"Wait. You want to be tied to a bed with no underwear? What's wrong with you?" I huffed in return.

"What! Are you from another planet? You know people play like this, don't you? It's just fine."

I must have been from another planet if this was what everybody was doing for sexual excitement these days. Not that I don't know about bondage and S & M, but I just didn't know it was so popular with the populous.

"It's not so fine doing this under the same roof where his wife lives," I said, stepping up onto my soapbox.

"She's not going to be his wife for much longer. *I'll* be his wife and this will all be mine. I won't be chained to a bed on the third floor then. Ha."

"How old are you? Do your parents know what you're up to?"

"How old are *you*? Too old for Dun, that's for sure. Is that why you're sneakin' around?"

"You think in that pea brain of yours that other women would want to slip between the sheets with Dun Wonderly because he's got money? Other women would rather drown themselves in pig poop than sleep with that nasty man."

"That's a hoot. Unless you're born rich, you marry rich, everyone knows that."

There was no sense arguing with her, but I was thinking of poor Sugar. If he didn't divorce her to marry this wastrel, I thought I'd prod her along. "I hear Dun has no real thought of divorcing Sugar and marrying you. He wants to hold on to his money as much as you want to spend it. I sincerely doubt he's going to part with it, since you do exactly what he wants."

"He can't live without me," she said, pouting.

"Just like he couldn't live without all the others for all those years he and Sugar have been married. He didn't divorce her for any of the others;

what makes you think he's going to divorce her for you?" I was going out on a limb here, but a sturdy limb that would hold my weight.

"And if you mention to Dun that I was up here, I'll tell him that you said you were marrying him for his money. Up to you." Then I turned walked out the door.

Coming down the stairs, I caught sight of Dun coming through the living room, probably on his way up to the third floor to dominate his greedy young girlfriend.

I hugged the wall, slipping into the downstairs bathroom to avoid him, and heard him humming to himself as he made his way up the stairs. Hi Ho Hi Ho, it's up to whip I go. I can't help it, that's what went through my mind.

Marilyn, bless her heart, had filled her plate to feed two, and was sitting at a small table in the library off the dining room with my two Wonderly sales reps, Rob and Linda. What a nice surprise.

"What have you been up to?" Marilyn asked.

"No good, of course."

"What do you know about Dun's young girlfriend?" I asked Rob and Linda.

Rob: "She's young and hot."

Linda: "Gladiola? Can you believe that name? She's a money-grubbing moron."

"I'm going to grab a plate and a fork, but I'll be back to hear more," I said. My stomach was growling. Snooping works up a hearty appetite.

Once I had my plate, I scooped up some food from Marilyn's. Instead of the pheasant under glass I was expecting, the food was all deep fried. Not that I minded the hush puppies and fried okra.

"So, seriously, what do you know about them? Is he getting divorced to marry the young girl?"

"How the hell would I know," Rob yawped.

"You never know with Dun. He's unpredictable," concluded Linda.

"I think this would be a good time to stop talking about Dun. See those big hulking guys walking around? They're not waiters," said Rob. "They're his bodyguards."

"Bodyguards? Does that mean he's in danger?" I wondered aloud.

"No, but everybody and anybody who crosses him is in danger, so maybe bodyguards isn't the right word. I'm not sure what they are," Rob said, looking over his shoulder.

"What about Bucky? Does he have money?" I asked what was clearly a tacky question "Why does he work for Dun Wonderly, anyway? He treats him like shit."

"Who knows? Maybe he just likes the perks of working for a place that sends him to Hollywood a few times a year to schmooze with the executives. And he loves the video conventions in August, where he rubs shoulders with some of Hollywood stars," explained Linda.

"Why wouldn't Dun do that, himself?" I inquired.

"Anybody's guess," Rob said.

"I'm going to the ladies room," I announced. This time not to hide, but to rid myself of three glasses of champagne. Or as Sugar would say, "My eyeballs were floating."

Vivian Henderson was sitting on the stairs, waiting her turn to do the same, and there were two women standing in front of the door waiting as well.

I sat on the steps next to Vivian and re-introduced myself in case she had the same ailment as her husband, Bucky.

"Hey again, Vivian. Annie Fillmore."

"I remember," she said pleasantly. "I know Bucky acts like he doesn't remember who he just met, but he puts up a good front for Dun. Dun doesn't care for anybody who is craftier or smarter than he thinks he is," she added, tilting her beautiful head. The red hair, the dark eyes, and flawless skin were captivating. "I ask Buck all the time how he stands it, but he just brushes it off. Dun Wonderly is terrible to work for. Uh oh, the champagne must be talking."

"Don't worry about it. I've had more of the bubbly than I need, too. I *have* noticed Mr. Wonderly isn't too nice to your husband, and it's disturbing, even for an outsider like me."

"He's horrible. I think there's something wrong with him. He lusts for everything: women, money, power, revenge, food. Oh, my goodness, I shouldn't be saying this, I've never said this out loud before. I hope you're not one of his spies," she said fearfully.

Not only was she lovely, she looked athletic. As I looked closer, I saw that her calves were molded like a sprinter's and her arms had a muscular tone. The strong manicured hands held a black satin clutch with a cream monogram to match her dress: vHw.

"Does your middle name start with a W," I asked, to make conversation.

"No, my maiden name, Ward."

"Oh. A detective friend of mine in Cincinnati is a Ward, too. I wonder if you're related"

"I doubt it. There are thousands of Wards in the area," she said dismissively. "A detective? I hope you're not working for Dun and gathering information."

"Heavens, no. I'm only here for the convention, and now I seem to be in the middle of what happened with Jessica," I explained.

"Why are you in the middle of it if you're just a customer?" she asked

"Because I had dinner with Jessica at The Wonder the night she died. Really, too long a story to tell right now, and it looks like you're up," I said gesturing toward the open door of the guest bathroom.

Luckily, she was quick, as I badly needed to get rid of the champagne.

Time for me to go to bed, I thought. This has been a long day and a longer night before. Neil's kiss was lingering on my lips, and I wanted to go to bed and dwell on that before I slept for ten hours.

"Anybody driving by The Dunbar soon?" I asked Rob and Linda when I returned to the table.

"You girls need a ride? I'm about ready to call it a night, too," offered Rob. "You'll have to scrunch in the front seat unless one of you wants to sit in the pick-up bed."

"Uh, no thanks. We'll scrunch," Marilyn said.

Rob went for his car while Marilyn and I waited on the curved veranda. No car jockey for him. As we were waiting, I heard a commotion behind us through the open doors. Vivian was having it out with Dun, stabbing his chest with her finger in what seemed like a tongue lashing. How much champagne *did* she have? I wondered where Dun's muscle was. Still guarding the stuffed pig? But Vivian didn't seem to threaten Dun—he was even smiling. What's more aggravating than being mad at someone and having them laugh in your face?

Marilyn shoved me into Rob's truck first, so I got to sit between them…being short has its drawbacks. A lot of drawbacks.

"Hey, what does Vivian Henderson do for a living? Does she work?" I asked Rob as he started up his truck.

"Yeah, she's the marketing director. Dun hired her from a hot shot marketing agency in Louisville. That's how she and Bucky met…when she moved to Wonderly."

"You goin' home tomorrow?" Rob asked.

"Yep, headin' outta town," Marilyn replied.

"How about you?" he asked, turning to me, "You going back to Briartown, too?"

"Sadly, no. Chief Earl told me this morning I have to stay until, I guess, they rule me out as a suspect."

"You're shitting me, right?" he exclaimed.

"I shit you not," I answered.

"Do you want me to hang around until all of this is over? I can if you want an ally. You don't know anybody else down here," he offered. "I'll just have to hide away from Dun. You know he likes us out there making money for him. He hasn't figured out yet how to implant a chip in us so he knows where we are at all times," he said, laughing.

"I hate to ask you, but it would make me feel better. Obviously, I didn't kill Jessica."

"Can't take more than a few more days. Sure, I'll stick around," Rob declared. What a gent.

Marilyn took the stairs to 239 like a high stepper in a Busby Berkeley film as I dragged myself up like the tortoise heading for the finish line. "Ya okay?" Marilyn asked, looking down at me over the railing.

"Fine," I managed to get out.

And as is life, Marilyn was snoring gently two minutes after lying down on the quasi-comfortable bed, while I was wide awake, frazzled and needing sleep way more than she did. But it didn't come.

CHAPTER 18

Around midnight I got up and asked myself what I could do with this time. Maybe a visit to the warehouse, I thought. Why not? I had the PIN 48531... was that right? I had written it down in my notebook, but I didn't want to awake sleeping beauty by rooting around for it. It was twelve thirty-five according to the clock. So off I went in my pj's to the warehouse.

I stretched my neck around the wall overlooking the lobby. Nobody was at the registration desk, or if there was someone there, I figured they were sleeping. My heart was pumping again as I crept down the stairs. As I arrived outside the door to the salespeople's desks, a golden rectangle of light splayed out on the floor from the hallway to Dun's office, where I heard loud voices. Hunching over, I made my way closer to the warehouse, but so I could still hear what was being said.

"You owe me fahv hundred k that's what it is. You've owed it to me for fahv years, and I want it paid up in full," bellowed Dun.

"I'm going to pay you Dunster, you know that. I'm your brother, I wouldn't cheat you," said the unmistakable voice of Andy.

"Cheat or not, we have a contract that you're pissing on. I don't take that crap from no one— and especially not you. Driving around in fancy cars with fancy women like you made that money yourself. It makes mah blood boil. That's on me all that good stuff you got."

"You have plenty of good stuff yourself, Dunster. But running a horse farm isn't as easy as you may think. The expenses are crazy. I'm taking to mowing the place myself to save money to pay you back," Andy kind of whimpered.

"You coulda paid me back some of it when you bought those two cahs," Dun reminded him.

"Well, you know you have to put up a good front if you want to attract the right customers. I board some of these horses for good money. These people aren't going to board their beloved horses with someone who doesn't look like they're successful. You surely get that," pleaded Andy.

"Don't give a damn. I want at least two-hundred and fifty k of that money in mah bank account in two months. If not, I'm gonna take the farm. Ya get that? I'll run that horse farm to make money, not to peacock around town. And don't fohget, I hold the mortgage on that land. I know you're payin' me, but it's mah land."

"This will get settled, Dunster, but you may not like how I go about it. Think about that," Andy said with a bit more gumption.

"Whatcha gonna do, Andy? Hard for me to think you're smart enough to figure out how to get that money and hurt me at the same time with that little brain of yours," Dun rudely pronounced.

At that line-in-the-sand statement, I heard thumping steps in the short hallway, and I dashed as fast as I could to a cube out of the line of sight.

I curled up underneath a desk and got comfortable, because who knows how long a feud between brothers can take. Perhaps I dozed off for a few minutes, because the first thing I remembered after that was the lights had gone off and I heard a door slam.

Figuring fifteen minutes was enough time to stay hunkered down, I watched time pass on a little red-colored digital clock on the desk.

The warehouse was going to have to wait until the next evening.

When I got to my room, the light was on and I heard voices. My first thought— of course, because I catastrophize—was that someone had entered and hurt Marilyn thinking it was me. But once I got to the door I realized it was Rob and Marilyn talking. It was one fifteen. What the hell was Rob doing in my room at that hour?

"Oh, my God," Marilyn screeched as she came toward me with her arms outstretched to give me a hug. So unlike her. "Where have you been? I thought you'd been abducted."

"Never a dull moment with you, Ms. Fillmore," the obviously annoyed Rob interjected.

"I'm so sorry. I couldn't sleep, so I went down to check out the warehouse. I didn't get a good look this afternoon, so I thought I'd try when nobody was there. But Dun was in his office, and I sure didn't want him to know I was nosing around, so I had to hide under one of the desks until he finally left. Does he always work at night?" I asked Rob.

"How the hell do I know what Dunbar Wonderly does when I'm not around, and frankly, it's none of my business," he belched out.

"Something's funny about him working so late after a big wingding affair at his house, don't you think?" I asked whoever wanted to answer.

"He can't be arrested for working late, Annie. You're going a little crazy with this whole thing, don't you think?" Rob asserted with hands on hips.

"There *is* a dead young woman, and a guy who was killed in the room next door. Right here. Do you think that's overreacting? I don't."

"Come on, Annie, let's get some sleep," Marilyn said pulling me toward the bed.

"I sure as hell hope you're alive when I see you next," Rob said making his way out the door, shaking his head.

Who could blame him?

"Why are you awake anyway?" I asked Marilyn as I lay down on the bed.

"I heard the phone ring and thought you'd pick it up, but when you didn't I turned the light on and saw that you were gone. The only person I kind of know is Rob so I called him in a panic."

"Who was on the phone at this hour?" I wondered aloud.

"I didn't answer it, but that little red flashing light might be a message," she said.

I couldn't listen to a message at this hour or I definitely wouldn't sleep. What kind of message at midnight or after can be a good message? And I was way too tired to tell Marilyn about Dun and Andy.

Oh, but for God's sake, I forgot to whisper—and Dun would get an earful when he listened to the bug in the room…wherever the hell it was.

CHAPTER 19

When I awoke the next morning at about 10 a.m. Marilyn had gone home to Briartown. She left a note on the bedside table: *Thanks for the memories and the murders. Get out of town before it's too late, my love.*

Wait, was she quoting Cole Porter?

After I read Marilyn's note, I picked up the phone to listen to my message. It was Alice Bostick asking me to go to her house that morning. She had something important she wanted to tell me.

I called Alice and let her know I'd be there by noon.

Having nothing else to do for the moment but find a bug in the room, I called the store to see if:

1. If it was still standing— it was;

2. I was making any money— more than Chicken Video; and

3. Everyone had turned up for their shift—they had.

As happy as I was that the store was still afloat, I felt a twinge of envy that it wasn't me keeping it buoyant.

I had breakfast downstairs and went back to my room to search for a bug. It wasn't in the smoke detector or in any of the lamps. Where else do they hide these things? After the fruitless search, I set off for Alice's.

Wonderly was becoming my natural habitat, and I wasn't sure I liked it. Could I actually live in this town all day every day with, maybe, a few thousand people I'd see on and off for the rest of my life? No. I was a city girl, not a country mouse. That day I hoped I wouldn't be living there until the end, but it being for just a few days, I rather enjoyed the hominess of it all. People shopping in the small retail shops reminded me of growing up in Castleton. Suburbs all across the country have lost this pleasant sense of community. Now it's Walmart at the end of a main street populated with empty stores that used to sell what Walmart now sells cheaper.

Alice Bostick was standing at her front door in perfectly ironed jeans and a blue striped shirt when I arrived. The flowers that had been scattered on the walk and porch had been cleared, and a swept emptiness took their place. Although perfectly coifed and fresh, Alice looked as depleted as her entryway.

She took my arm, looked left and right at the door, and pulled me inside.

"Ty's back in town," she whispered.

"Isn't that kind of dangerous for him?" I inquired.

"Yes, of course, but he told me he can't move on until Jessica's murderer is found. He said his only wish is that he could find him first and kill him himself."

"Where is he? Where's Ty?" I asked.

"I told him about you, and he wants to talk to you. I don't know why he wants to talk to you and not me, but I think he has something to say that he doesn't want me to know," she said, her eyes moistening.

What seemed most likely was that he didn't want to put Alice in harm's way, but I was expendable, he didn't know me.

"He said he'd be at the pump house on the lake at twelve-thirty, and he'd like you to meet him there."

A pump house? The only time I'd been in a pump house was when I was hiding from a boy who I thought wanted to kiss me when I was about ten years old. My Moms had rented a cottage on a lake north of where we lived. It was bliss swimming in that lake and picking water lilies along the water's edge. The kid who I thought wanted to kiss me was a skinny red-headed boy with pale blue eyes and bad breath. He ran after me on my way home from camp one day, and I ducked into a pump house that was slick and green with moss inside. I didn't think he'd follow me but he did, and after he entered I turned my back to him in the slimy corner and covered my eyes. That's when he slipped a caterpillar down my shirt—and the beginning of my poor judgment of what men want. And my only experience with a pump house. But back to Alice.

She brought me a glass of water in an amber goblet just as she had done on my first visit, and we sat as we had before. The awkward silence filled her spotless home.

"Have you heard from Mr. Wonderly again?" I asked to fill a bit of the space.

"I haven't heard from him directly, but two of his, um, people stopped by with flowers and a big check. I felt funny taking it, but these guys didn't look like they were going to take no for an answer."

People? I'm thinking henchmen, bodyguards, crew for the capo dei capi, the Kentucky mafia.

At about twelve fifteen, Alice said, "Why don't you start out for the pump house? I don't want Ty hanging around too long. He'd be easy prey for anyone who might see him."

"Of course," I complied. Ty was like her son. Just that one sentence gave it away.

I took off down the bumpy street toward the lake. Even though I could see it clearly, it was probably about a quarter of a mile down the muddy dirt road. My yellow Chuck Taylors weren't going to be yellow for long.

When I got to the sandy, rocky beach, I looked left and right for what I hoped to recognize as a pump house. Why didn't I ask Alice where I would find it? I walked to the edge of the green-grey water and looked again. To the right and tucked back amid some weeds was a grey clapboard house that had to be the pumping station. Where were they pumping water? There didn't appear to be any cottages along the lake that I could see...maybe a relic of some past weekend getaway for people from Lexington and Louisville. I had a brief vision of people frolicking in the lake with nineteen twenties bathing suits and umbrellas to shield their milky skin. That vision seemed delightfully innocent, and so unlike the present-day mess I was finding myself in.

By this time my nifty sneakers were caked in wet mud, gritty sand, and other flotsam and jetsam, and for a moment the state of my favorite shoes overtook my lust for finding out what happened to Jessica. That was short-lived once I knocked on the pump house door and entered.

Some version of Brad Pitt was sitting in the corner on a barrel. The light was dusky, but I could still make out his hooded blue eyes and prominent lower lip. As he stood up to greet me I pegged him at six foot three. His navy blue sweatshirt slipped off his shoulder, and when he bent over to retrieve it, his muscles rippled under a tight grey T-shirt. Rob was right, this kid could have gone off to Hollywood with Jessica to take a stab at stardom.

"Are you Annie Fillmore? I sure as shit hope so," he said in a light southern cadence.

"Yes," I said offering my hand for a shake, "and you are Ty."

"Yes, ma'am."

"Let me say how unbelievably sorry I am for you and Alice. You know I had dinner with Jessica on Friday evening, and I liked her so much."

"She was drunk. Did you like that?" he asked.

"Well, she was a bit tipsy, but she had a rough day so I understood."

"She's not a drinker. Wasn't a drinker," he said, lowering his head, "and she couldn't hold it. We had an argument at the Wonder bar. I wanted her to go home, and she wanted to sit and get drunker."

"Well, as I said, she did dine with me. She seemed okay when we finished before she walked home."

He took off his black baseball cap, revealing long blond wavy hair. Looking down, he fidgeted with the cap, while nervously tapping his boot on the dirt floor.

"I have to tell someone this because I'm pretty damn sure it's what might have gotten Jess killed."

"Okay. You can trust me," I said prodding him on.

"I can't tell Alice, and I hope to God she never finds out," he said bending down and pulling over a wooden crate that he upended for me to sit on. He sat back down on the barrel, and I waited for him to speak again. I was looking up at him as if in adoration, but it was that my head was going to explode if he didn't tell me what he came here to say. He clearly wanted to tell me something but was having trouble getting it out.

"Why don't you just tell me?"

"Dun offered me ten thousand dollars to have sex with Bucky, and I took it. There, that's the kind of asshole I am. My dad's an alcoholic, and I take care of all the bills and him and our house, so that was the incentive—to get out of debt, or almost out of debt anyway."

He didn't look at me.

The crate I was sitting on wobbled, because I wobbled. He really needed that money.

"Why on earth would Dun want you to have sex with Bucky? Did he say?"

"Shit, no, he didn't say. But he must have wanted something on him for some reason. I don't know the ins and outs of the workings of a fucked-up mind like Dun Wonderly, but he didn't spend ten K for nothing, that's for sure. And I was just a big enough idiot to go along with it, to help out the worst guy I've ever known."

"Did you? Did you lure Bucky into sex with you?" I asked.

"Yes." That's when he started crying.

"That was the worst of it," he continued, "because Bucky's a good guy, just a yes man to that cocksucker for some reason. Sorry."

"And you told Jessica this the night she died?"

"What the hell was I thinking? She'd had way too much to drink, and I thought she'd take it better with alcohol in her. But I had to tell her; it wasn't right not to. She had stars in her eyes about the two of us going to Hollywood and making our mark. All *I* wanted was to move out of Wonderly, have a few kids, and live happily ever after."

"What was her reaction?"

"She said the weirdest thing. She said, "Wow, I guess what Bobby Crane said is true."

"Did she tell you what she meant by that?" I prodded.

"No. All she said was, 'we're going to be rich baby, we're outta here.' "

"You had no idea what Bobby Crane said to her, or what made her think she was going to be rich?"

"I thought she was drunk and was rambling on as she sometimes did."

"What do you think she was going to do at the warehouse?" I questioned.

"I didn't know until the next day that she went to the warehouse, but my guess is she thought she'd blackmail Dun, and he killed her. Or had one of his thugs kill her. A small town like this seems so innocent, but my experience in Wonderly tells me it's not. And when you have someone like Dun as the head honcho, it's even worse. Evil follows evil. To give you one small example, last year when Jack Hardesty had a fling with one of the sales reps…" he continued.

"Who's Jack Hardesty?" I interrupted.

"He's one of the warehouse crew who works for me. Anyway, at one of our monthly meetings, Dun said, 'I hear Jack Hardesty's getting' a little pussy from Isabella. Don't you know, boy, you don't get pussy in your own cat house?' "

"He said that in front of everybody?" I asked, aghast.

"Yep. That's who he is."

"Were Jack and Isabella at that meeting?"

"Not for long. They up and walked out, and Dun suspended them without pay for two weeks."

"What an asshole," escaped my lips.

Trying to get back on track, I asked, "What did Jessica actually have on Dun to blackmail him though?"

"I'm not sure, but I think it must have been the thing that Bobby Crane told her."

"Was she naïve enough to believe she had the clout to blackmail someone like Dun with all of his thug bodyguards?"

"She was naïve like that, yeah. She really wanted to leave Wonderly and become famous. Working in the entertainment business in Kentucky puts stars in your eyes. She's not the only one that wanted that, maybe not to be a movie star, but to work for one of the studios, and that's entirely doable.

A few people from Wonderly do work for the studios. But she wanted to be another Julia Roberts. She was drunk that night and could never handle the booze."

"So let me get this straight, you think Dun Wonderly had reason to end Jessica's life?"

"Right," he said finally, looking me in the eye.

"This is a lot to digest, and that's what I'm going to have to do—sit with it for a while, let it sink in. There are some obvious red flags, but I've known red flags to turn out to be red herrings."

"Red herrings? What's that mean?" asked Ty, now standing.

"Never mind. It's just an expression. You're not staying in this pump house are you? Somebody's sure to sniff you out, don't you think?"

"No, I'm not staying here."

"Where *are* you staying?"

"There's an amazing cave system in Kentucky, those that are known and those that are unknown. I'm staying in one that's unknown."

"How do you know about it if nobody else does?" I asked.

"Thirteen-year-old boys may be the greatest scouts in the world, and not just the Boy Scouts, the rest of us. There's just about anything we'd do for an adventure, and anyplace we'd go to find it. God knows how some of us didn't die; falling off cliffs, getting stuck in mud, being bit by bats that we didn't know were rabid or not. Jesus, it's a miracle we survived. We did find caves that Indians must have known about, but we never saw any sign of anybody being there besides us. Even later when we'd take a girl over there, nada…just our own footprints."

"So you're going to stay in a cave?"

"Have been staying. Nobody'd ever find me. I'm confident of that."

"Okay. I have to say this doesn't sound good for you with Dun being the kind of a slug everybody says he is, but I'm gonna try to help you in any way I can. I'm not a detective, but I'm clever in an eavesdropper kind of way. You're not above finding caves when it puts you in danger, and I'm not above meddling when it puts me in harm's way. Let's leave it at that. I guess I should speak with Alice if I find out anything? Of course, I won't say anything to her about you and Bucky."

"Thanks, Annie. Can I call you that? That's what Alice calls you."

"Yes, Annie. Again, I'm so sorry about Jessica."

"Nothing's going to bring our Jess back, but somebody's going to pay, that's my only wish right now, revenge."

"I might sound like your mother, but don't do anything stupid. You're being in jail for the rest of your life isn't going to make Alice feel any better. Please, think about Alice, and what's your father going to do without you?"

"Yeah," he said, kicking the dirt floor, "Yeah, you're right. But we have to find out who did this."

The door creaked when I opened it, and I peeped around left and right to see if anybody was in view, but the coast was clear so I slogged along the sand to the muddy road back through the little village to 239 to think.

But on second thought, I was starving.

CHAPTER 20

Buckling under to my hunger pains, I stopped at Momma's Grocery, the last shop on the main street. I needed a sandwich, and not one made by The Dunbar Hotel.

As soon as Momma's door opened, held by a kind gentleman in a cowboy hat, the small-town grocery smell hit me. What is it? Soap? Something waxy? Whatever it is, it's inviting, and an odor that all small grocery stores seem to share.

Luckily, they had a meat-and-cheese counter, and the guy wrapped in a white apron and matching shower cap around his beard made me a ham and swiss on rye with mustard. Well, not bread *I* would call rye. It was like brown Wonder Bread.

Once I was settled back in my room, munching on the sandwich, the quality of the bread was of little consequence, because what I really needed was to digest what Ty had told me.

Whatever Bobby Crane told Jessica might have gotten her killed. What the hell was it? And maybe it got Bobby Crane, himself, killed. Two deaths in the same place are just too coincidental to be for different reasons. I could be wrong. I am so often about so many things, but this nagging feeling about it made me think I was right. This was like one of those two thousand piece jigsaw puzzles, all I could find were the straight perimeter pieces. What I needed were the exasperating interior ones.

The next, and seriously wise, thought I had was that I needed some sleep. I might have slept five hours the night before, and I'm one who needs a good eight hours to be able to navigate the world with a straight mind. The clock said two fifteen, so an hour's nap would hopefully take the edge off.

Groggily pushing through the sleep, I knew I had to get up. The clock read five thirteen, so I did, indeed, get my eight hours' sleep that day. Five o'clock meant it must almost be time for dinner. Maybe I'd try the BBQ place with the mutton, not that I would have eaten the mutton. I rolled over, picked up the phone, and asked for Rob Woodbury's room. As luck would have it, he picked up.

"Are you hungry?" I asked.

"I'm always hungry," he answered.

"Would you like to dine with me tonight at the barbeque place?"

"Yeah. Last meal before I leave town. I have to head over to Lexington for a new Blockbuster franchise. Or at least I'm going to try to pry them away from their current distributor. So you'll be on your own, is that okay?"

"I'll be fine, I'm sure." But I sure wasn't sure at all.

"Good," he answered.

"Well then, a little mutton is just what we might need. Meet you downstairs in about fifteen minutes?"

"Be there or be square," he said. Such a boy scout.

I didn't have time to take a shower and wash my yellow sneakers so I just washed my face, put on a dab of makeup, and figured the jeans I was wearing would do for a barbeque joint.

Thank heavens I had my Doc Martens. Otherwise I would have had to wear heels with my jeans and look like a hooker. I know some women wear jeans and heels, but not me.

Rob drove his pick-up truck around the The Butt Hut parking lot three times before he finally found a spot in the back. The building was long, low, and red brick. People sure liked barbeque in these parts if the restaurant was as packed as that parking lot on a Monday night.

The Butt Hut was written in fancy gold lettering on the glass front door, and through it I could see a black-and-white tile floor.

"It's going to be every man for himself finding a table," Rob shouted as he opened the door to the clamor of the crowded restaurant. "Do you mind sitting at the bar? That might be our only choice."

"Don't mind at all," I said.

"I'll catch us a few seats. Why don't you check out the buffet to see what you like?"

There were spare ribs, lamb chops, chicken, beef, mutton—none of which looked appealing to me lounging in their aluminum trays. Maybe I'd just order a salad.

Rob found two seats nearest the door at the end of the bar and had already ordered a beer for himself and a white wine for me.

"What do you like?" He asked

"In general, or at the buffet?"

"Buffet."

"Nothing. I think I'll have a salad; all that meat in one place makes my stomach roil."

The bartender called the waitress over to take our order. Good grief, it was Gladiola.

"I think I'll just have a salad. What kind of salads do you have?"

"Salad? That's a side.

"Okay, I'll have two side salads on one plate," I ordered

"That's a side. That's not a dinner."

"So I can't order two sides?"

"Let me check," she said, rolling her eyes walking toward the kitchen.

Rob looked at me and shook his head. "Can't you do anything normal?"

"Well, you're from Indiana. I'm from New York. That's two different normals. And, I *am* your customer, let's not forget that," I said, eyebrow raised.

"Right now you're more of a pain-in-the-ass friend who's buying videos from me," he chortled.

"In what restaurant in the world can you not order a side salad as your main course?"

"In this one," he laughed, the beer loosening him up.

Gladiola came back to us,

"What kind 'a dressin' you want with that *salad,*" she said, with so much emphasis on the mixed greens.

"What do you have?"

"Italian, French, blue cheese," with another eye roll.

"Blue cheese, please."

"You?" She looked at Rob.

"Buffet."

"Boy Howdy," she said as she trounced away.

"Lots of training for the staff I see," I said to Rob.

"Drop it," he cautioned.

Rob excused himself to get spare ribs, baked potato, and corn from the buffet. Those spare ribs did look kind of good, but there was no going back now. Gladiola slammed my order of two separate side salads down on the bar before she sashayed away in a huff.

Most of the rest of the evening was me and Rob hashing out video business, a little gossip, and a few laughs.

The door kept opening and closing, and opening and closing... but at one point it just opened and didn't close. At the door stood two guys dressed like the thugs at Dun's party. For all I knew it might even have been them. They stood there until Gladiola came up to them and gave them each a hug; then they followed her around for the rest of the time until Rob and I left.

"Protection for Gladiola from an order of a side salad?" I asked rhetorically.

CHAPTER 21

Back at The Dunbar, Rob and I said our good-byes at the bottom of the steps. "I'll call to make sure you're still alive, or you call me if you need anything. I'm staying at a Hampton Inn off of seventy-five," he said.

Climbing those stairs was the only butt-building exercise I was getting that week. But to get to Bare Bottom Babes quality, I'd have to climb the stairway to heaven.

Nine-thirty was too early for sleep, so I again I considered what I knew and what I didn't know. While deliberating, I took a shower, washed my hair, dried off, and grabbed a clean pair of pj's. I didn't know who killed Jessica or Bobby Crane. At least I was clear on that. The hell with it, I grabbed my John D. MacDonald paperback, *Dress Her in Indigo*. Where I wanted to be was curled up on my couch with Travis McGee under the throw Helen crocheted for me—with a delightful single malt Scotch nearby. But here I was in an outdated hotel in Kentucky with a tattered paperback mystery, thinking of real murder. Then I fell asleep.

The alarm clock said 11:46 p.m. when I awoke, but it sure felt like a new day. Now I was wide awake again with nothing to do.

Looking for bugs in room 237 didn't appeal to me. Maybe it would be a good time to check out the warehouse again, but only if Dun wasn't in his office. I could creep down there and check just to waste some time until drowsiness overtook me again.

Should I change, or go down there in my cozy flannel pj's I wondered? Cozy flannels it was. I stepped into my Chuck Taylors, which I had washed and which dried nicely, took my teeny *What About Bob?* flashlight, and took off for the warehouse. Of course, I checked the front desk to make sure I wouldn't be seen, and once again the coast was clear. There must have been a roll-away bed down there.

Poison permeated the air of the sales room, and it was hard not to think of Sugar and the scent she wore at the party. The room was dark. The door to Dun's hall and office was closed, so unless Sugar was hiding under one of the desks as I had the night before, she must have been there that day. Either that or someone else was wearing that overpowering stuff.

I entered Linda's PIN, the lock unlatched, and I rolled the hefty door open just wide enough to slip through, leaving it open just a crack. Once inside, I clicked on the flashlight. I had no idea what I was looking for but was hoping something would jump out at me. The warehouse was back to pre-Jessica's death condition, shelves looming in the darkness like those massive Moai heads on Easter Island.

The shelf on the end that held the Bare Bottom Babes and Wet T-Shirt videos was as erect as it was before it fell on Jessica. I walked to the other side of it where, presumably, it had been pushed. What was I looking for? The police had already checked the whole place out, so I wouldn't find anything that they hadn't already seen. And yet ….

I moved around each shelf and shone my little light on the contents, hoping I'd see an empty space from where Jessica took the video she was holding when she died. But there were lots of slots where videos had been taken for customers.

I proceeded like this up and down the front of each shelf until I got to the back of the warehouse, when the overhead fluorescent lights switched on.

"Hey, who's in heah? Anybody heah? For Christ's sake these people are as useful as a trapdoor in a canoe." Dun.

I jumped into one of those canvas mail caddies on wheels and covered myself with canvas bags as I heard footsteps coming toward the back of the warehouse, and I stopped breathing.

"Jumpin' Jehoshaphat," is all I heard him say as he walked right in front of where I was nestled in the caddy. He stopped for a second or two, then walked around to the other side, clicked off the lights, pulled the door to and locked it.

Oh great! I was closeted in the warehouse in my pajamas until someone opened up in the morning. How did I get myself into these predicaments?

Concrete floors do not allow for a good night's sleep, but I did my best. I made a bed out of as many canvas bags as I could find, laid down on them, and covered myself with a few more. I slept for heaven knows how long before I heard the outside door heave open and saw some hazy daylight filter through the cavernous warehouse.

Why hadn't I thought of what I was going to do at daylight when someone opened that freezing barn? Boldly walking out in full view of whoever opened the warehouse wasn't an option, so I skulked around the shelves until I was within two units from the delivery door. A man walked down the center aisle toward the inside door to the sales desks and tapped in a PIN, giving me an opportunity to make a beeline for the back door. I ran around the outside of the warehouse like a running back, a running back in pink-and-white striped pajamas. And what an idiot I was not to realize I could have tapped in Linda's PIN into the pad and gotten out of there last night.

Pushing my back against the outside wall, I inched toward the front of the building, but as I was slinking, I saw what looked like Andy Wonderly's Corvette parked in the grass across from the warehouse. What was Andy's car doing there at this time of the morning? But more importantly, how was I going to get to my room? Surely not in the 'Vette. Perhaps I'd find a side door to the hotel, maybe even the one from which I think somebody removed the body of Bobby Crane; but the two doors I attempted to open were locked. Did I have the guts to walk into the lobby of the hotel in my pj's? What choice did I have? I did see a guy going through the breakfast buffet in his bathrobe the other day. Who'd even notice?

As I rounded the corner of the building, a police car pulled up and stopped with a screech in front of the hotel. As the two officers entered, I followed close behind them, scooted through the lobby, and tore up the stairs as fast as Marilyn had done the night before. I plopped on the bed, peeled off my sneakers with my toes, and looked forward to finishing up a night's sleep.

The phone rang.

CHAPTER 22

"My mothers? Here? In the lobby? Okay, I'll be right down." Oh boy, they must be on to something.

I stepped into my jeans, threw on a T-shirt, laced up my Doc Martens, and went downstairs to say hello and find out what they knew that I didn't.

By the time I got to the top of the stairs, the lobby was crawling with police—and my two Moms. Helen's pale blue raincoat and hat blended nicely with the officers' dark blue uniforms, while Emilie stood out in a voluminous black wrap topped with a fuchsia hat adorned with a yellow feather. Was Kentucky ready for this?

"Darling, my darling," Helen said as she enveloped me in her five feet of love.

"Annie, you look tired," said the much more pragmatic Emilie as she too gave me a hug, "and I'm sure you'll tell us why you came in the front door in your pajamas this morning."

"Oh, you saw me. What the hell is going on here? What are all the police here for?" Hoping, wishing, praying it wasn't anything I did or was thought to have done.

"Officer Hines over there said," inclining her head in the direction of five police officers, "there was a death that might be suspicious. But, it wasn't suspicious; it was murder," Em declared with confidence.

"Who? Who died?" I asked, almost shaking by that point.

"It seems to be a cowboy of importance," said Helen. "The officer said something like this wasn't his first rodeo, and it sounded like he was a big cheese. Is there a rodeo in the arena?"

"It's one of their funny terms, 'this ain't my first rodeo' meaning he's no rookie, meaning it has nothing to do with cowboys or rodeos," I tried to explain.

"Oh dear," said Helen.

"Someone's dead, and it's someone important," announced Emilie, "And what does all of this have to do with you?"

"Let's go up to my room. I'll order some breakfast, and I'll tell you all about it," I offered.

They were carrying their huge suitcases from the 1950s, so I dragged over one of the brass bellman's carts and put their cases on to take them to my room.

The ladies loved the glass elevator and oohed and aahed the one flight up, and when we alit and were walking to room 239, Helen said, "And look at these lovely window boxes hanging on the railings, aren't they fun, Em?"

"Oh my, yes," agreed Em.

"When was the last time you two have been in a hotel? This place is kind of shabby, don't you think?"

"Isn't it on purpose?" asked Helen.

"Isn't what on purpose?"

"The shabby part. You know, shabby-chic?"

"I'm pretty sure it's just old and worn out," I said, "and time for a refurbishing. But here we are. I'll order breakfast and give you a blow-by-blow of what has happened over the last few days. You're not going to believe it," I said.

"We'll believe it," they responded in unison.

The phone was ringing as I was about to pick it up to order room service.

"Annie, it's Linda. Have you heard?"

"No. The lobby is filled with police, and I know someone died, but that's all I know. What's up?"

"Dun Wonderly was found dead in his steam room this morning. I can't tell you any more now, but we have to meet so I can fill you in."

I was as shocked as one of those dead pigs with his snout in an electric socket... or something like that.

CHAPTER 23

I collapsed back on the bed, and was instantly surrounded by the two people I needed the most, Helen and Emilie. Thank God, they were here.

But then I wondered aloud, "How did you get here?"

"We flew into Louisville, took a puddle jumper to a little place in the middle of nowhere, then someone was kind enough to drive us here," said Emilie, patting my hand while Helen was soothing my brow.

"When you recover, Annie, tell us from the beginning. We'll try to contact the Guides to see if they can help in any way," Em exhorted.*

*"I'm okay to tell you now." And I did. I told them everything that had transpired since Friday when I arrived, as Em took notes in her black-and-white composition notebook—the kind we used in elementary school.

"So that's it. Any thoughts you might have would sure help because I have to get back to the store. I've been away way too long. Oh, and while you're here, if I don't have time, maybe you can check out room two thirty-nine to find bugs. I've checked the lamps, smoke detectors, TVs, radio, telephone—but nothing. If there is a bug in room two thirty-seven and

---

* Helen and Em describe the Spirit Guides as non-physical entities that help each of us guide our thoughts and spirits away from negativity and back to love. Some of us have one Guide, some a whole bunch. I had a hunch mine looked a lot like Doc Brown trying to get Marty McFly back to the future.

nobody's removed it, the murder of Bobby Crane might be recorded, so we would know who murdered him—and maybe Jessica, and now Dun Wonderly. If it was one person who murdered all three of them."

"Okay, dear, we'll do our best. But now I think we should register and get to our room so you can eat your breakfast and get a nap. Surely you didn't sleep on that warehouse floor," announced Em.

"Good, you register, and I'll bring your bags to your room. Then I'll sleep."

After taking Moms' luggage to their room, I returned to 239 and sat by the window thinking about the insane news that Dun Wonderly had actually been murdered. Just like you, dear reader, I thought he might have been the culprit … now what? It didn't, of course, mean he didn't kill Jessica, but it did mean there was still a murderer on the loose.

The phone jangled as I was about to pick it up to order food.

"Meet me in front of the hotel. Is your car parked in the lot? We can talk safely in there," Linda instructed.

"I'll meet you in there in ten minutes."

The lobby was swarming with police, Wonderly personnel, and nosy guests. In the middle of that assemblage stood Daisy Dixon in an orange jumpsuit, yellow heels, and her standard gold nugget necklaces. She looked like she was ready for a prison close-up.

I hotfooted it down the stairs with my head down, trying to avert recognition, and dashed through the lobby to the exit where Linda was waiting for me.

"I can't even remember where I parked, it seems like years ago instead of a few days," I whined.

The parking lot had thinned out, since a lot of people had left that morning (not being murder suspects, or Daisy), so it was easier to spot my silver Honda.

Once I unlocked the car and Linda and I were seated in the front seat, she turned and looked at me, not saying a word.

"What?" I asked. "That terrible?"

"Have you ever seen someone who's been murdered?"

"Yes," I responded.

"But not Dun Wonderly. Nude," she said, and started shaking.

I leaned across the gearshift to put my arms around her, but it was an awkward hug with that thing sticking in my boob.

"I'm so sorry you had to see that. But *how* did you come to see it, Linda?"

She sat forward in the seat and said, "I found him. I had a big order for a chain store customer, and I wanted to be sure it was right, so I went in at seven to pull the order with Jack Hardesty, the guy who's taking over for Ty. I noticed Dun's outside door was open, which is unusual because he doesn't get in until about ten. His office door was open too, which is even odder. Then I saw the Kentucky Long Rifle stuck in the steam room door handle. That's when I ran to get Jack." She exhaled, slumping back in the seat.

"Oh no," is all I could get out.

"When Jack got there, he pulled the rifle out of the handle, and when he opened the door Dun's buck naked body fell out into the office from the steam room. It was so awful I just want to bleach it from my memory." And she started sobbing. "I don't remember anything else until the police came."

"Didn't they want to talk to you immediately?" I asked. "I mean surely they wanted to ask you questions."

"Those were just the uniforms, the chief wasn't there yet. I'm pretty sure the chief is going to ask me about how I found him, ya know? So they said I should hang around, but I figured talking to you was still hanging around. I haven't left the premises."

"What's this all about?" I wondered aloud. Although, I did know at least three people who might have wanted him dead, maybe more. He wasn't exactly Mr. Popularity.

"I have no idea, I'm pretty sure I'm in shock, but I'd better get back in there to see if the chief wants to question me. I may never recover from this," she moaned.

"You'll get over it. It might take a few weeks, but you will," I soothed.

Then Linda got out of my car and ran back into the hotel.

My car had been sitting there for five days, so I figured I'd better take it for a spin down Pleasant Street to warm it up a bit. The engine started to turn over when I started it, but it fizzled out before it caught. The odometer read almost 99,000 miles, and nothing had been wrong with it for all those miles, so I wasn't surprised—bummed, but not surprised.

Helen and Em were in room 337, directly over the room in which Bobby Crane met his end, and I hoped that wasn't bad luck.

But I needn't have worried. When I knocked on their door and heard the simultaneous "Enter," I also smelled a lovely aroma. They were gently waving sage smudge sticks around the room while incanting, "Cleanse this hotel and make it clear, only good may enter here!"

I started to back out of the room, but Em stopped me. "No, dear, you may come in. The sage will do you good as well. After we finish clearing the room, we'll work on you."

I envisioned my toes on fire from the smoldering smudge sticks. What were they going to do to me with those things? The only thing I needed at that moment was something to eat, since I spoke with Linda instead of having breakfast.

"This is all dandy, but I'm starving, and my car won't start."

"Of course, Annie, darling. Let's order room service for you. Then we'll see to your car. And, of course, we'll release any bad energies around you," said Helen, coming over, with the smudge stick way too close to my hair as she bent down to kiss my cheek.

Em said, "We can recite the release prayer with you, Annie, while we're waiting for your food. Why don't you order now?" she asked.

So I did. Two eggs over easy, extra bacon, English muffins, fruit bowl, biscuits with extra butter and jam, and as much coffee as they could bring.

Helen asked, "Ready dear?"

"Do I have to do anything?" I asked petulantly. Why do I sometimes revert to my childhood self when I'm with them?

"Just be open, honey, that's all," soothed Helen.

"I release all energies that no longer serve me, all negativity that surrounds me, and all fears that limit me. So it is," said Em. "That's all you have to say as the healing of the sage envelops you. Feel the negativity leaving you as the sage removes it from your aura."

I knew what an aura was because I was raised by these two zany characters—the energy field that surrounds us and is part of us. I knew they'd persist if I didn't give in and say their spiffy words, so I did.

My breakfast arrived just as the "removal" was done. Did I feel better? Yes, because my breakfast had arrived, and the sage smelled like we were sitting around a smoky camp fire about to eat s'mores.

After a breakfast fit for the likes of Red Neck Ricky, I went back to my room and called down to the desk to ask for the name of a reputable auto mechanic in town. The receptionist gave me the number for Uncle Dan's Dandy Repair. Seemed about right.

I called the number, and the person who picked up said, "Yeah?"

"My car won't start. I'm staying at The Dunbar Hotel. Can you pick it up and take a look at it?"

"Yep. Culah, make, model," he asked.

"Nineteen eighty-seven silver, Honda Civic." I threw in the license number for good measure, but I was going to be standing by it, so he didn't really need that.

"How long do you think it will be before you can get here?"

"Gimme twen'y minutes."

When I called to tell my Moms about the car being picked up, they said they wanted to wait with me and then take a walk downtown. I could show them the sites, such as they were.

They were waiting for me in the lobby when I walked down the stairs, and I wasn't disappointed. Emilie looked like she was ready for the hunt, wearing a red riding jacket over a long black skirt that covered almost all of her black boots. Her round black hat had a fluffy bow at the back and was pitched forward over her dark brown hair. Astoundingly dark for her age. She says it's natural. Helen's rolled eyes tell a different story.

Helen was in the same blue raincoat and hat as she was wearing earlier that morning, but she had added a pair of snazzy blue-suede cowboy boots that had some kind of brown swirly motif on the sides. They looked smashing.

I had thrown a black jacket over the T-shirt, so people may have thought I was their chauffer.

As Em forged ahead toward the car, I asked Helen where Em got the outfit and if she had bought it just for this trip to Kentucky.

"Oh, she didn't buy it, dear, she made it. Yes, she made it the night before we left. Isn't she amazing?"

"Always, and always surprising. Like she knows just where to go to find my car."

"Wasn't that the car we were in last year when we visited?"

"Yeah, but still."

"She's at the top of her game, dear. Could be the brewer's yeast and blackstrap molasses she eats every morning when we're home."

While we stood assembled at my car waiting for Uncle Dan, Helen said, "It was lovely flying in over Kentucky this morning, all the trees and vacant land. You don't see that flying out of LaGuardia, do you?"

"No, Queens is not Kentucky, that's for sure," I said, "but sometimes I miss New York City's crowded streets and all that buzz."

"Oh yes, all the conflicting energy in one place can make for an intriguing day," chirped Em. "But one must surround oneself with white light as protection when in large crowds. There was a lot of negative energy here in that lobby this morning—anxiety and negativity. No wonder we could sense trouble for you, Annie."

Uncle Dan pulled up in a battered yellow tow truck advertising Uncle Dan's Dandy Repair in black lettering on the door, with his telephone number underneath.

"Dan?" I asked sticking out my hand for a shake.

"Dandy," he replied shaking my hand with his big meaty one. "Mah real name's not Dandy, but tha's wha' people lahk, so tha's wha I ansa to."

"Okay, Dandy."

"Yaw keys in ta ignition?" he asked.

"Oh no, " I said, fumbling in my black bag, and handed them over to him.

"See? People 'ways wantin' their'n cah done in a minute, but neva haf ta keys where it twoud make it quicka," he said getting into my car shaking his head.

He did what I had done earlier, turned the ignition just to hear it fizzle out.

"Alternata'," he said with confidence. "Seems ta be a lotta cah trouble at The Dunbar taday. Ha' to tow Andy Wonderly's bran new cah in early ta' mornin' with some affliction."

"Andy's car? Where did you have to tow it from?" I asked, knowing exactly where.

"Roun' back ba ta warehouse."

"What was it doing back there?" I asked brazenly.

"Now lada, I don' ask mah custama's wa they pahked where they'n pahked, I jus fix the damn thins."

Reasonable answer.

"You wan' a rebuilt alternata or a new one?"

"What's the difference,"? I asked.

"One's new and one's an ol' one rebuilt," he said, taking his cap off and scratching his head.

Sparse grey hair covered his bespeckled pate. He seemed to be bespeckled from head-to-toe with what surely was grease. His ruddy face was especially lubricated with it.

"What's the difference in cost?" Em asked.

He looked up as if this is the first he noticed two other women standing with me. "Hail, a'll hafta let ya know. Ya wan' me ta ca' the hotel an' let ya know?"

"We're walking downtown now, maybe stop for lunch. Are you located near downtown?"

"Ya know where The Butt Hut place is?"

"Yes, we may eat there."

"Ahm right roun' back of tha' place. If ya spit out tha back winda of the Hut, you'll hit ma gah'rage."

"We'll stop by after our shopping to see what you found and how much it'll be, then we'll have lunch. How long do you think it will take?"

"From staht ta finish, 'bout an are' and some. Unless I find sumpin' else needs fixin."

"Thanks, Dandy, see you in a bit." I said.

"My goodness, Annie, I'm so proud that you can speak his language. Where did you learn that?" asked Helen after Dandy was on his way with my car in tow.

"Hit or miss, Mom. If I know the subject, I can hang in, but if I have no idea what they're talking about, they might as well be speaking in Swahili."

CHAPTER 24

"Ready for our walk?" asked Em, linking her arm in my right arm as Helen linked hers in my left.

"And, we're off to see the wizard, the wonderful Wizard of Oz. We hear he is a whiz of a wiz, if ever a wiz there was…" and so off we sauntered down Pleasant Street.

"Oh, my goodness, Em, look at that—Boo-Kay. Isn't that clever? That must be the Kentucky way to say things, so quaint," Helen said, clearly dazzled by what I thought was downright silly.

"Charming," agreed Em.

Stopping in Tom's Pharmacy for some talc that Em had forgotten, reminded me that I had ruined my Glade Country Pottery Air-Freshener when I clocked my intruder. But by this time I was either used to the smoky pollution or it had dissipated. I'd have to get the ladies to sage the room. It was still smoke, but far healthier.

My Moms lingered with delight at Wittler's Antique Mall. The more delighted they became with each and every item, the antsier I got. I can waste a good amount of time in one of these places, beguiled by things I had when I was a kid that I wish I still had, like the full set of *The Bobbsey Twins* books. But that wasn't the time. I needed like hell to get back to my own store. After stopping at almost every booth, they ended at the jewelry counter where Marilyn must have bought my cameo set. Between Helen and Emilie they probably could have filled another counter themselves with jewelry from the boxes and boxes in their bedrooms. Yet they still had an appetite for more.

"Annie, do you see anything that catches your eye? I'd love to buy you a trinket to remember our trip," Helen cooed.

"Do you see a skull and cross-bones pin?" I asked cheekily.

"Oh you," Helen chided.

They weren't leaving empty-handed. Em chose a large starburst crystal broach with five different colored stones. Helen decided on a pair of Trifari pearl-and-gold clip-on earrings. They both only wore clip-ons. It hurt my earlobes to think of it. How their ears weren't down to their shoulders after all the years of wearing those leaden treasures, I'll never know.

By the time we left Wittler's, it was after noon. Helen and Em were hungry. Even though I had just downed a breakfast fit for a lumberjack, I was game for lunch.

"Would you like to try the barbeque place near Dandy's shop? We can stop and see if he's had a chance to look at it and if it actually is the alternator," I suggested.

"It's the alternator," they responded as one.

It was another half-hour before we actually arrived at Dandy's shop, because we stopped at Delilah's Candy's (they each bought a little box of chocolates), Finery Boutique (no purchases), Derby Saddlery (Em bought a pair of "peddies" with a black foot and flowered upper that could reach your knee). Mercifully we bypassed the cleaner and the plumber.

"Mom, exactly what are peddies?"

"They're socks to protect your feet when horseback riding, dear. The ankle is padded to protect rubbing, as are the heels. Most necessary."

"I didn't know you rode."

"Oh yes. I've taken up riding in the last few years, maybe more. So bracing to get out in the fresh air. And, of course, the horse is my spirit animal. Mr. Larry and I have become very close."

"Mr. Larry?" My eyes were wide-open now.

"The horse I ride every week. We've had lifetimes together before, so I was naturally drawn to him," she said proudly.

"But, of course," I answered.

"Mom, do you ride?" I asked Helen.

"No, I don't, but I've taken up bocce ball and table tennis. Quite exerting, especially the table tennis. It's a senior league. Such lovely people."

Why was I surprised? They were never ones to sit and watch television for hours on end. "Up, up," was their war cry—even when I was trying to watch *The Cisco Kid* in the afternoon.

Arriving at Dandy's about twelve thirty was perfect timing for lunch directly afterward.

Uncle Dan's Dandy Repair was a ramshackle garage that surely hadn't been painted in twenty years—maybe ever. But his lot was full, and he and two young guys were bent over what looked like Andy Wonderly's Corvette.

"Hi, Dandy," I called out.

"Hey," he returned.

"Was it the alternator?"

"Tha's wot I sad, raht?"

"How much to replace for a rebuilt or a new one?" I asked.

Em came forward, "She'll take the new one."

"One fifta," he answered.

"Fine," Em answered.

"Um, do I have a say?" I asked.

"It's our little gift to you," they both said, standing together, arms hooked.

"Thank you so much. You really are the best mothers a girl could ask for," I said encircling them both in my arms.

"Okay, Dandy. A new alternator. How long do you think it will be?"

"Ya havin' lunch?"

"Yes, at the The Butt Hutt,"

"Stop back," he said, turning to walk into his garage.

Okie Dokie.

"So you ready for some mutton?" I asked jokingly.

"Mutton, well now that will be a treat," said Em, heading toward the copse of trees that separated the garage from the restaurant.

When I swung open the gold-lettered glass door, the noise from the diners was again loud.

"How much fun," said Helen, not giving a thought to how we weren't going to be able to hear ourselves think.

As we stood at the host stand, waiting for someone to seat us, I scoped the place out for Gladiola. Sure enough, there she was bustling at one of the back tables.

"Good afternoon," said the host. "We're mighty busy, but I think I can find a table for you three lovely ladies. This way, please."

We followed the waddling Terry, as his name tag indicated, to the back of the restaurant. I didn't need my Moms' psychic abilities to know that our waitress was going to be Gladiola. This will be good, I thought.

We sat at a table with a banquette. Helen and Em sat on the banquette side, looking out at the other diners. I sat across from them on a chair, looking at them and a wall. Sure enough, Gladiola came over to us with three large menus that were sticky to the touch. Not looking at me, she asked my Moms if this was the first time they'd been to The Butt Hut.

"Oh yes, and we're so excited to try your mutton," chirped Helen.

I know it's wrong, but I almost wanted to pinch my beloved mother like I used to pinch Iggy when she'd scream her head off in the supermarket cart because I wouldn't buy her a five lb. bag of candy.

"You're in luck, 'cause I hear it's extra good today," Gladiola crowed.

"In that case, we'll have two orders of the mutton. And what comes with that?" asked Em.

"You can choose whatever you like at the buffet," she said, pointing to the enormous food bar in the middle of the restaurant.

"What about you?" she said snarkily with a side-eyed look. "Side salad?"

"No. I'll have the buffet as well."

"Yippee," I heard her mutter as she turned and left.

"She's a pretty little thing, isn't she?" complimented Helen.

"Picture her chained to a bed waiting for her sixty-seven-year old lover," I snapped.

"Oh dear, that's who that is? Poor girl, so misguided," commiserated Helen.

"We all are where we are, Annie. No need to judge her. She'll evolve, if not in this life then in another," Em explained.

I had to remember that—people aren't assholes forever.

Having Gladiola as a waitress was a tradeoff for much better acoustics in the back of the restaurant due to the overhang we sat under. We actually could hear each other and converse.

"Shall we go to the buffet to see what they're offering with the mutton?" asked Helen.

"Good bread, good meat, good God, let's eat," I quoted, remembering a grace I used to say to their consternation.

"Oh you," Helen said.

As we stood on line for the grub, I peeked ahead to check out the mutton. No way could I eat that. It had been cooked so long to make the tough meat edible that it was falling off the bone.

When our turn came, Helen and Em grabbed their heavy cream-colored crockery plates and piled on mutton, coleslaw, and potato salad. I piled the ribs on my plate, along with potato salad and coleslaw—my preference for Germanic sides must be genetic.

Em tucked into her mutton first. "Oh my, perfectly gamey as I had hoped."

"Yes, Em, and the vinegary coleslaw complements it so well," tittered Helen.

Two satisfied customers. Well, three, because the ribs *were* succulent.

"So after we finish lunch, we'll go check on my car," I said.

"Did you see they have a dessert bar, too? We can't miss that," murmured Helen.

Where do these ladies put all the food? They weren't skinny, but they definitely weren't over-weight. Maybe more horseback riding and bocce ball for me.

I sat out the dessert, but they came back with two that they shared—some banana concoction with whipped cream on cake, and a warm berry cobbler with vanilla ice cream on top.

Gladiola came with the bill. Em paid, and I noticed she left her a generous tip. That might have made up for the side-salad affair.

CHAPTER 25

As we walked back through the stand of trees to Dandy's garage, I noticed Andy Wonderly talking to one of the mechanics.

"That's an interesting looking gentleman, Annie, don't you think?" asked Helen.

"Interesting? If you mean he's good-looking, yes. But I've met him, and he's not interesting to me.

"Oh?" Em asked, cocking her head.

Andy looked up as we approached the garage. "Howdy, I know you don't I?" he asked me.

Yes, we met Sunday night at the hotel bar, and then you drove me and my friend, Marilyn, to Dun's party."

"Ah must be befuddled because of the awful news this morning. Ah guess you heard 'bout my dear brother."

Dear brother?

"Yes, we were at the hotel when we heard. I'm so sorry, Andy. May I introduce my mothers, Helen Weidner and Emilie Gloeckler."

"Your mothers? You have two?"

This is precisely why I don't like introducing them as my Moms, but it would have been shoddy if I didn't give these two their due.

I explained how when I was three my two aunts adopted me when my parents died. I hoped he wouldn't want more details. I didn't like him well enough to share them.

"Ahm so happy to meet you lovely ladies."

"Thank you, dear Andy. We are so very sorry for your loss, but rest easy that your brother is in a good place," comforted Em.

Really? I wouldn't have guessed that. I was thinking more like a long sentence in purgatory while he learned a few lessons. But what did I know? What does anybody know?

"You are ever so kind. I do hope I'll get a chance to spend a little time with you before you go home. Where is home?" he asked.

"New York. We're from Brooklyn originally, but now we live in Castleton, a suburb of New York City. You must come visit," said Helen.

Say what?

"You dear ladies are making this terrible day so much better. I'd love it if you'd join me for tea at my home if you have time this afternoon." The words oozed out of him like sorghum syrup.

"I believe Annie's car is finished, so we'd love to join you," cooed Helen.

"Ma' car won't be ready 'til later. Perhaps you can drive me home and I'll show you the farm. It's wonderful Kentucky country where my home and the stables sit. And I'd love to introduce you to some of my beloved horses."

"How perfect," said Em, clearly enthralled with Andy Wonderly.

"Emilie rides, you know," Helen confided.

"Well then, a spin on one of my horses is a must today, madam," he said bowing his head toward Em.

"Lovely," Em responded.

After Em settled the bill with Dandy, I drove the three new best friends out of the garage lot and took a few left and right turns to what soon became horse country. I stopped listening to the ingratiating conversation from Helen, Em, and Andy, and enjoyed the countryside. I did manage to spit out, "Andy, what was your car doing in the back of the warehouse this morning?"

"Back of the warehouse? Why, why ahm not sure," he stuttered.

"I saw it there while I was taking my early morning walk today," I lied.

"Ah yes, now I remember. I'd left it there the other night when Dun and I met in his office and he offered to drive me home because I had trouble starting the 'Vette."

I knew that was a lie, because I was hiding under the desk as he stomped out of Dun's office by himself. And did he call his car the 'Vette? Yuck.

The ladies went silent after that. They knew what I had told them about the heated conversation between Andy and Dun a few nights before.

Andy's farm was not what I was expecting. I was thinking something grand like The Magnolia Plantation in Charleston. His home was more like a bungalow.

"Shall we have tea first, or would you like to ride?"

"Just Em rides," I said. "Why don't you two have a trot, and Helen and I will walk around a bit. May we go in your house if we need?"

"My home is your home, my dears. Please feel free to use the powder room and make tea if you'd like, or coffee if you prefer," he said appealingly.

"Em, do you prefer astride or sidesaddle?"

"Oh my, you have sidesaddles? That would be perfect."

As I looked at her in her riding outfit, I wondered if she actually knew she'd be horseback riding on her visit to Kentucky. That would have made sense because her costume was over the top even for her. And let's not forget the purchase of the peddies. Maybe she gazed into a crystal ball before their trip to Kentucky.

Andy and Em walked to the stables to choose a horse for Mom, and Helen and I started in the opposite direction. A lovely road wound around the acreage enclosed with white wood post-and-rail fencing. I felt like Elizabeth Taylor in *Giant*. Although Andy was handsome, he wasn't Rock Hudson handsome.

After about twenty minutes, Helen decided she needed the facilities, and I wondered if a little snooping wasn't in order.

Andy's home had a distinctly masculine vibe. Directly across from the front door was a fireplace over which hung a huge deer head. The dark brown leather sofa and matching chairs coordinated with the nose and eyes of the dead deer. Helen found the restroom as I roamed around the first floor, where I found a small kitchen with adjourning dining area. The square cloven-hoof dining table, over which hung an antler chandelier shouted, "I'm manly."

Off of that was a pretty backyard. On the patio directly outside the door sat a round table, with four chairs and a red umbrella growing out of the middle.

An office completed the downstairs. And that's where I headed, the office. A large mahogany desk messy with papers sat in the center of the room, which was lined with bookshelves. I quickly flipped through the papers on the desk finding nothing but bills. Then I tried the drawers. A crumpled piece of paper was stuck in the back of the middle drawer. It was a note from Dun to Andy dated Monday, October 21.

Andy, as previously stated, I want my money in my bank by December 21. Hear? No more monkeying around. I'm dead serious. Dun

Well, that note was damning, wasn't it? I thought for a moment of taking it, but I came to my senses before I actually stuck it in my pocket.

Were the police going to interview Andy? Somehow I'd have to let them know that he and Dun had a serious monetary squabble.

As it turned out, I needn't have worried.

"Annie, Annie dear, someone's knocking on the front door," Helen informed me as she found me in Andy's office.

I opened the front door to Chief Denny Earl. "What the hell are you doin' here? You seem to be everywhere," he blustered.

"I know, it's crazy," I agreed. "We met Andy at the garage where my car was being fixed, and he invited me and my mothers to tea."

"Yeah? Where is he? I need to speak with him," he said starting to come into the house.

"He's riding with my other mother, Emilie Gloeckler. They both ride," I explained so stupidly.

"Okay, we'll check the stables," he said walking back down the path with a uniformed policeman in tow. But he turned around to say, "If he comes back here before I get to see him, tell him not to leave."

"Yes sir."

Helen walked back into the living room, sat down in one of the leather chairs, and let out a prolonged sigh. "Oh dear, what can the police want with Andy?"

"You picking up any murderous feelings in this house, Mom? Can you tell if he might have murdered his brother?" I boldly asked.

"There is an undertone, dear, but I'm not sure it's murder that I feel. It's something quite dark though."

Could have been the taxidermy wall décor.

Then the door swung open to reveal Em backlit by the sunshine, which illuminated her like a shorter Auntie Mame after the hunt. Her hat was cocked forward on her head even farther, almost covering her eye, and her jacket was slightly askew.

"Are you okay," I asked rushing to her side.

"Dandy, dear, we had an exhilarating ride."

"Did Chief Earl find Andy?"

"Yes, we were dismounting when he found us. It's all fine. Naturally, Andy will be interviewed; it *is* his brother who met his end after all," she said decisively. "They're on their way over here now, so we should leave, we don't want to interfere." It was like she was covering for her lover. Good Lord.

We drove back to The Dunbar in silence. It seemed nobody was in the mood to make merry.

Once parked in front of the hotel, I said, "I really need a nap. It's three-fifteen, how about if I nap and you do whatever you would like. Then I'll meet you in the lobby at, say, five-thirty? Maybe we can have a cocktail before we decide about dinner; but that was a big breakfast and lunch, so not too much for me."

"Indeed, not too much for us, either, dear. Is there a small restaurant at the hotel? Or we could do room service if it's available for dinner," Helen suggested.

"We can even order a pizza I imagine," Em piped in.

We bid our farewells at the elevator with hugs and kisses. We even hugged and kissed when one of us would go out for a loaf of bread. Because, you know, you never know.

I left a wake-up call for four thirty because as much as I needed sleep, a shower and hair wash were necessary too.

After the snooze and shower I was getting ready for an early night with my Moms when I noticed the red light blinking on the phone. The message said, "Annie, it's Alice Bostick. Can you call me when you get a chance? The sooner the better."

The time was five twenty-three, so I made a quick call. "Alice, Annie Fillmore."

"Thanks for calling back so quickly, Annie. I met Ty at the pump house this afternoon and told him about Dun. I assume you know?"

"Oh yeah, I heard."

"He's kind of freaking out because he's afraid he'll be a suspect even though, of course, he didn't do it."

Of course.

"I can see why he'd be worried, Alice, but he's out of harm's way for the moment, right?"

"Yes, I guess, but he'd like to see you again."

"My Moms are visiting from New York, so I'll have to figure out a good time for me to get down there by myself. Can I call you back tomorrow? "

"I guess that will have to do. We do appreciate all the time you're spending on this, but we're anxious, you know."

"Of course. I'm happy to do what I can, but I don't know what that is right now except listen and collect information."

"Okay," she said, "talk tomorrow."

My Moms were ready in the lobby all dressed up in a change of frocks when I trounced down the stairs. Em, out of costume now, was swathed in navy; Helen in pink.

The bar was not nearly as crowded as it was on Sunday when Marilyn and I met Andy Wonderly. We were seated at a table near the front. The noise swelled around us like a wave, but I was able to see who was there, so I was content.

"Might have to go to the bar to pick up drinks, if you both would like a drink?" I offered.

"Scotch, neat," Em said.

"A little white wine with some seltzer, please, darling," Helen requested.

Scotch, neat? Did I know this was Em's drink? I'm sure I would have remembered. Maybe, I thought, that horse ride was more than she was letting on.

"Mom, did you always drink Scotch, neat?"

"Not always, but I've acquired a taste, and there's no reason to sully it with water or ice. Not for me, anyway."

Do we not pay close enough attention to our parents to know that a tea drinker might, one day, turn into a Scotch drinker? I've learned so much about these two surprising women. As much as I loved them as mothers, I now admire them in ways I couldn't have foreseen.

Indeed, I did have to go to the bar and scrunch between the bodies on the crowded stools. Happily, one of them was Linda Chambers, drinking something clear white in a tumbler.

"Linda. Hey."

"Oh, my God, what a day. I may just stay here all night. Tim can take care of the kids until I sober up. I was in with Denny Earl, the chief, for about an hour. How could I tell him anything more than what I saw in a few minutes, but he dug and dug and dug."

"My Moms and I took my car to be fixed at Dandy's, where we met Andy Wonderly. Surprisingly, he invited us to his house for tea, and we pretty much spent the afternoon there. I have some info about Andy and Dun, but I don't know how to tell the police. I overheard stuff and I'm not sure I want the chief to know how I heard it."

"You mean how much Andy owes Dun, and that Dun holds the mortgage on the farm? Everybody knows that; not a secret. I guess that's all past tense now. Anyway, you don't have to tell the chief anything about what you know about those two. He knows it all. We all do."

"Whew," I said.

"One of the reasons I was with Chief Denny so long is that someone used my PIN to get into the warehouse last night. We all know each other's PINS, but why at that time of the night? I couldn't seem to talk him out of believing I was there. But I have a solid alibi, being at home with Tim and the kids, and my Mom and Dad came over for dinner. So, hopefully, that puts me in the clear. And maybe they can tell from fingerprints," Linda expounded

Gulp. Of course I should have told her right then and there it was me. Something stopped me. Guilt? Shame? Chicken-shittedness? Probably all. Oh boy, fingerprints.

Back at our table I noticed Em sipped her Scotch as it was meant to be sipped, slowly. Helen barely touched her wine spritzer. I drank my Scotch on the rocks and had another.

The rest of the evening passed without incident, unless ordering and eating a pizza in a hotel room counted as something.

"I'm going to meet Ty Patton tomorrow morning after breakfast. Can you two entertain yourselves," I said as I was leaving their room.

"Rest assured we will find something entertaining," said Helen.

"More than entertaining," added Em.

CHAPTER 26

Light peeked around the heavy curtains when I awoke at seven thirty, a sure sign of a sunny day because any light penetrating that room meant the sun was blazing.

At 8:30 I was dressed and ready for breakfast and then, if it's what Alice wanted, off to meet Ty at the pump house. Descending the stairs, I was not at all surprised to see Helen and Em already going through the buffet.

Their plates were piled high with everything the buffet had to offer— even the goetta; a meat-and-grain sausage or hash said to be of German inspiration that's popular in Cincinnati. But as Dun Wonderly advised me when I arrived, Cincinnati and Wonderly were kind of the same neck of the woods. Not being as active as them with horses or bocce balls, I went lighter with an egg and a slice of bacon.

"I won't be long; I'll definitely be back for lunch. Would you like to have it here or venture out again?" I asked them.

"Why don't we see how long you are actually gone? Then we can make a decision," Em reasoned.

"And what do you think you'll do this morning?"

"We'll check out the room for bugs and hope to find something," said Helen. "Did you notice the headboards are bolted to the walls? It could be behind there if they were very wily," she speculated. "We'll continue to work on it."

Em was busy with her goetta and didn't look up, but I knew she was cogitating.

We lingered over breakfast, savoring the moments together. We chatted and laughed until about nine-forty-five. After we said our good-byes I went back to my room to call Alice to see if it was okay for me to meet with Ty. How did she and Ty communicate if he was living in a cave? Smoke signals, carrier pigeon?

"Alice, it's Annie, I'm on my way if it's a good time."

"I'll let him know. He'll be in the pump house by the time you get here."

Driving seemed like a better idea than walking that day. My car needed to keep moving I figured, and I wanted to get back to my Moms as soon as I could.

By the time I was parked in the small lot where Rob had parked when he first took me to Pleasant Lake, it was about ten-fifteen. I slogged through the sand again to the pump house. Ty wasn't there when I arrived, but I chalked it up to the difference in time between my driving and walking.

But after forty-five minutes I figured he wasn't coming. I left the car where it was and walked to Alice Bostick's house to find out what was going on. Alice was pacing on her front walk.

"What's up?" I asked.

"You won't believe it. Ty was on his way to meet you when the police picked him up."

"What? Where was he when the police found him?"

"In the woods in back of the houses across the street. He spent the night here last night, got cleaned up, and hoped you'd be able to meet him.

You didn't say anything to anybody, about where he was going to be, did you? Somebody must have alerted the police that he was here."

"No, of course not." Well, I did tell Helen and Em but they wouldn't say anything to anybody because they didn't know anybody except Andy. And they still wouldn't have said anything to him. No way.

"What grounds did they have to pick him up?"

"I don't know. I just saw the police car inching down the street, then one police officer got out, ran between the houses to the woods, and about fifteen minutes later out he came with Ty, and put him in the back seat. My heart almost stopped."

"You think he's innocent, Alice. Let's just hope they know what they're doing, and he'll be released and be able to go back home instead of living in a cave."

"But I've watched so many cop shows on TV and they just want to arrest someone to close the case, you know?" she said, wringing her hands.

Alice thought Ty was innocent, but did I? Ty had a damn good reason to think Dun had killed Jessica ... and maybe he did kill her. I sat with Alice a bit more because she was so agitated, she seemed to need company. I wondered if she really had any doubts at all about Ty's innocence even though she professed her confidence in him.

These were my thoughts as I drove back to the hotel to the comfort of my Moms.

I spotted them right away sitting in the lobby restaurant, talking to Sugar Wonderly, who was looking decidedly un-widow-like. Her white dress with sprightly yellow flowers matched the yellow straw hat tipped rakishly over one eye.

"Good afternoon or is it still morning," I greeted them as I pulled over a chair from another table.

"Hi, Annie, sweetheart. Just a hair after twelve," said Helen. Em also said good afternoon as well as Sugar. But Sugar didn't call me sweetheart.

"Ty Patton was taken by the police this morning," I announced.

"Ty? What for?" asked Sugar.

"I guess he's under suspicion for murder of Jessica, Dun? Both?" I guessed.

"Gracious me, Ty? That's just catawampus. Ty didn't kill anybody. For Lord's sake someone has to help him out."

"It doesn't seem like that young man did anything bad," Em said with her eyelids at half-mast.

Helen shook her head from side to side in consent.

"Your Moms have been telling me about their connection with the other side. I'm so fascinated. They're coming to my house for tea this afternoon to read the Tarot cards for me. Please come along, Annie," Sugar invited.

"I'd be delighted," I responded. But I was thinking, is this what one does after their husband has been murdered in his steam room. Have their Tarot cards read?

"Shall we order lunch?" Helen asked.

A waitress sped to the table when Sugar raised her hand in the air. Her burgundy-blue-and white striped uniform was crisp even after the breakfast crowd. Her brown hair was tied neatly in a high pony tail. "I'm so sorry, Mrs. Wonderly, for your terrible loss."

"How kind of you, Flora. How's the family? How's that little one of yours?"

"Goin' on eight now, so not so little," Flora answered.

"My how time does fly. So happy all is well with you and your family." Flora rested her hand on Sugar's shoulder and I noticed a slight squeeze. Everybody seemed to be family down here.

We all ordered BLTs on toasted white bread with coleslaw and chips on the side. And iced tea. Well, Helen and Em and I ordered iced tea. Sugar ordered "swee-tay," and Flora knew what she meant. When it arrived with our iced tea it looked exactly the same.

"Is that iced tea, Sugar?" I asked.

"Oh honey, it is, but with lots and lots of sugar. That's why we call it swee-tay," she said.

You can't know somebody very well from a few meetings, but the few I'd had with Sugar told me I'd insist on being her friend if she lived nearby. What the hell was Dun looking for that he didn't find in this delightful specimen of a woman?

Nobody brought up Dun until Sugar did, but, of course, I was dying to.

"Well, I guess we'd better clear the air and talk about that crazy old fool who got himself killed last night, or this mornin', or whenever," Sugar said.

"You think he brought it on himself?" I asked.

"A person doesn't act like a damn donkey to everybody and be cruel as a snake, and expect there'd be no consequences," she declared. "Karma has teeth."

"Yes, dear. But murder seems extreme, don't you think?" Helen asked, her hand reaching out, touching Sugar's.

"I had plenty of reasons to murder him, but I didn't. I know it's not considered by some to be rape if a husband rapes his wife. But I consider it rape, and he did that to me twice. The last time he tried, I bought a little revolver to keep in my bedside drawer. I told him I was going to shoot him if he did it again. And God knows he was nothing if not a coward. That was the last time he came near me for what he called his connubial rights."

"Why didn't you divorce him, Sugar?" asked Em.

"I should have. I had papers drawn up that I wanted him to sign, but as much as he would have liked to part with me, he liked less parting with his money. He knew I'd bleed him like a stuck pig. I actually stopped by his office last night to plead with him once more, but he wasn't there."

That explained the aroma of *Poison* in the air. "Have you any idea at all who could have done this? Who could have killed him like this?" I asked.

"Could have been anyone in town. Even me, but, as I said, it wasn't me."

"Perhaps something lighter now, conversationally," said Em. "We have an afternoon tea to look forward to, and a Tarot card reading."

Lighter meant commenting on our delicious BLTs with an umm or an ooh, but nothing else.

Dressing for tea in Kentucky called for flowered dresses and straw hats for my Moms. It was the black dress for me—a step up from jeans and a black T-shirt. I was going to burn that dress when I got home. If I got home.

Before we left for Sugar's and I was alone with Helen and Em, I asked them if they had mentioned that I had been in touch with Ty to Andy Wonderly, or anybody else they'd met.

"Come to your senses, Annie. Would we ever tell anything out of school about something you're involved in? Or anything in general? Never."

"Of course not. Alice was just wondering how they even knew exactly where Ty was."

"You said, 'houses across the street'? Surely there are people in those houses who know what's going on. Em and I know a lot that's going on in houses around us. We're observant of our neighbors as most people are."

Helen made a good point.

God knows, when I hear a loud noise from my next door neighbor, I fill in the blanks. Heart attack. Burglary. Kidnapping. Or maybe someone just fell off the bed in the heat of passion, although my neighbors are in their eighties.

CHAPTER 27

Cruising around Sugar's circular drive, my Moms where duly impressed. "And a fountain, oh my!" exclaimed Helen.

The door was open, so we knocked lightly, and Sugar came through the hallway to greet us. I wondered how long it would take her to overhaul Dun's gaudy, golden palace.

"Please come in ladies. Let's sit in my inside veranda as I call it. So much more soothing, don't you think?"

"Lovely," said Helen looking around. I wondered if she was taken in by all Dun's frippery.

Once seated in the cozy white sofa, Sugar said, "I've taken the liberty of making us mint juleps—so perfectly Kentucky for visitors from the north, don't you agree?"

Whether we agreed or not, nobody turned down the golden libations. They looked so pretty with the green mint crushed in crystal goblets.

"Here's to the broads," Sugar toasted.

"Hear, hear," joined in Em.

I was smiling from ear to ear. I sure hoped she wasn't the one who had done in her husband.

"Isn't this a wonderful room?" I asked my Moms.

"Ever so delightful," Helen agreed.

"Delightful," chimed in Em. "Do you entertain in here a lot? I would. So welcoming."

"I do have my girlfriends over a lot. We love to yuck it up and gossip about what's going on around town and even in Lou'ville and Lexington. We all have friends there, too. It's not that far. Have you been to Lou'ville, you must go," Sugar insisted without knowing whether we had been there or not.

"I can't leave town," I pouted.

"Our plane landed in Louisville, but we didn't have time to visit it properly," said Em, "but maybe on the way back we'll do that."

"Let me know, and I'll give you a long list of things you must see. I know a few friends who would be overjoyed to entertain you for lunch on a real veranda."

"Oh my, such lovely southern hospitality," Helen mused.

To get back on track, *my* track, I asked Sugar, "Are you friends with any of the women who work at Wonderly? The sales women, or Vivian Henderson?"

"I know them all, of course, but we don't hang out as I do with my friends who are more my age. Vivian and Bucky have been here for dinner and drinks many times, but that's hard. Or was hard. Bucky made Dun even meaner than normal, maybe because Bucky never said a word in his defense. And poor Vivian, if looks could kill, Dun would have been dead long before this. That's an odd couple don't you think? You have met them, haven't you, Annie?"

"Yes, I've met Bucky a few times, and both of them were here at your party on Sunday, so I did have a few words with Vivian. She's so elegant."

"Isn't she just? A lovely magnolia blossom in the midst of the rest of us drooping on the vine."

"Good grief, that's not true at all. Almost every woman I've met down here, including you, Sugar, is beautiful. Vivian might be dressed like a runway model, and her hair might be cut in a Vidal Sassoon style, but other than that she's no more beautiful than the rest of you."

"But she isn't like the rest of us. She doesn't fit in. She's guarded, not loosey-goosey like me and my friends. There's a difference I can't put my finger on. Not that she's not cordial, she is—but something's different," she confided. "Of course it could be that she seems so bewitched by Bucky, and we've all known Buck since he was a kid, so that's hard to fathom, ya know? But there's no doubt they're in love. For their fifth anniversary, Bucky gave Vivian his mother's antique pistol, complete with all the engraved bullets. It's unusable, of course, but it's the very idea he would part with something he holds so dear. He'd had it framed and keeps it in a place of honor over their fireplace."

Of course, we didn't know Bucky at all well—Helen and Em hadn't even met him—so this bit of background was interesting. And I did see Sugar's point. Vivian seemed like she'd be on the arm of Sean Connery not Tom Hanks. But, hey, love is funny and people are funny about who they love. I was struggling not to fall in love with a guy twenty years younger, so who was I to pass judgment?

My mint julep was down to the bottom mint leaves, Sugar's was gone, Em's half gone, Helen's barely touched. "Shall we have another julep, or are you ready for some tea sandwiches and coffee or tea?" asked Sugar.

"Tea sandwiches and coffee would be lovely," said Helen, putting her drink down on the table.

"We're not used to drinking in the afternoon, Sugar. Kind of rubes," I said, trying to not make her sound like an afternoon tippler.

"May we help with the sandwiches?" asked Helen.

"Not at all. Tessie will bring in the sandwiches. All coffee? Or would someone prefer tea?"

"I believe coffee for us would be great," I said, knowing at least Helen was going to need some coffee to offset the few sips of bourbon and sugar.

Sugar pressed what I assumed was a bell to the kitchen. Within a few minutes a tiny black woman with grey hair tied back in a low bun and wearing a light blue dress came in wheeling a cart with sandwiches. The dainty sandwiches were on a tiered server. A silver coffee pot with matching cream and sugar bowls and four delicate flowered cups and plates looked like they were from a spread in *Southern Living* magazine.

"Tessie, meet my new friends."

Sugar introduced us and said, "Tessie, you are a marvel. Thank you, dear. I hope you've saved some for yourself."

"I've been nibblin' while I was makin'. You know me, Sugar."

Like a magician, from her commodious pocket she pulled out four linen napkins rimmed with lace. She then placed them and all the goodies from the cart on the table.

"Thank you, Tessie," Helen, Em, and I said.

"Happy to do it. Happy to celebrate," Tessie said.

"Oh, Tessie, the ladies will think ill of us for celebrating someone's demise," Sugar chided.

"Ha," is all Tessie said before leaving the room.

"Has Tessie been with you long?" I asked Sugar when Tessie was out of earshot.

"She's been with my family since I was a teen. She's like a second mother to me—a smarter one. She's read the Bible about ten times; and just to make sure she knew what it was all about she read the Koran, the Talmud, and any other holy book she could get her hands on. And she remembers it all. She calls herself a Christian, but she says there's truth in all those other books, too. She can spot evil ten miles away. I think she can sense it really. We almost broke our ties when I married Dun. In the end, she thought I needed her more than ever. How right she was."

"Did she attend school?" Em asked.

"I don't know ... she doesn't like to talk about it. But today every kid in The Flats goes to high school and more. A few years ago a young black boy who graduated at the top of his class in Wonderly was the Valedictorian. Lord, you should have heard the outcry from certain idiots in this town. That a black boy was smarter than their white kids was more than they could take in. But he prevailed and also got a full scholarship to Harvard. Tessie and I were doing celebration dances all through the house."

A lull sat in the room while we absorbed this news.

I took a bite of the delectable lemony cream cheese and cucumber sandwich, and to change the subject I said, "Dun's death must be hard on Andy."

"Hard on Andy? Kind of like me, he's probably celebrating."

"Surely not," said Em.

"Like I said, not too many people are sorry to see a snake in the grass killed with a heavy rock. Maybe his money-grubbing toddler girlfriend, but eventually she'd want him dead, too. I do realize that's a terrible thing to say, but I'm just being honest," Sugar confided.

"I've heard Dun held the mortgage on Andy's farm, and had lent him some money for start-up. But surely that's not reason enough to kill him?" I suggested.

"That's just part of it. They've hated each other since the day Andy was old enough to stand up and Dun was mean enough to knock him down. Those old eight millimeter films show just how awful Dun was to his little brother. His mom had divorced Dun's father and remarried Abner Wonderly, and Andy was the result of that second union. For whatever reason Millie, Dun's mother, took Dun's side. On top of that when Andy was in his teens, it became clear that he was a knockout compared to Dun's unspectacular looks. Dun didn't care for that one little bit. And then, there was Dun's financial success that Andy was jealous of. Dun did work hard, but there wasn't a loop he didn't crawl through to get his way. He cheated both ways—when he had to pay, or when others paid him. He paid less and charged more. He's duplicitous, cagey, wily, the worst kind of cheat. So they hated each other. If you're wondering if Andy could have killed Dun, I'd say he could have as long as he didn't get blood on a new jacket.

"I know you're too polite to ask why the hell I married him, but I'll tell you he could be a charmer when he wanted to. And he wanted me, and charmed me off my feet. Every once in a while when we were engaged I'd see something that raised my antenna, but it was so short-lived I gave it no mind. I didn't know the real him until the honeymoon, then he became who he was—cantankerous and mean."

By this time we had made a good dent in the dainty tea sandwiches. There were three left when Tessie came back, "You ladiês want anything else? Something sweet?"

"No, Tessie," announced Sugar, "unless somebody wants some delicious petite fours."

The three of us politely agreed we had had enough with the sandwiches, and Helen asked if she could help clear the table with Tessie. "You being paid by the missus or am I?" Tessie chuckled.

As Tessie was clearing the table and putting the dishes and cups back on the cart, Sugar said, "Enough about my past, how about my future, ladies? I'd love my cards read now."

"Oh yes, let's get down to it," said Em, foraging in her commodious handbag for the cards, the Rider-Waite-Smith Tarot deck that she always used.

"Perhaps I'll take a little walk so I don't disturb the ethers," I suggested.

"How thoughtful, dear," Helen declared.

I made my way to the kitchen to find Tessie cleaning the dishes by hand. I'd taken a cue from her not to ask if I could help. "Hi, Tessie, do you think Sugar would mind if I take a little tour of the first floor?"

"Have at it. Sugar's going to get rid of this place and find something cozier once all the hoopla about Mr. Dun's death is over. Too bad the gardens are done for the year; they're something to behold. But you can still see a bit of glory back there. Go to the end of the hall and on the left is Mr. Dun's office. You can see from there how pretty it is. Or you can walk out the French doors at the end of the hall."

"Thank you, I'll take a little jaunt while Sugar finds out her future with the Tarot cards."

"What in the world is she doing that for? Scares the bejesus outta me to think about knowin' what's going to befall me," she kind of moaned.

Many people felt like Tessie about the Tarot, but I was so used to them they didn't bother me. There were times when cards foretold something less jolly than I'd like. But as my Moms tell me, we have free will so we can change the trajectory of our life by our behavior.

I haven't changed yet.

Dun's office was as expected—over the top. There was more ornate shiny gilt than a gold mine in Africa. The coldness of the décor with the gold and marble reflected what I had heard of his character—icy and soulless. The heavy, gold velvet drapes on the windows fell to the floor, held back with corded velvet roping that revealed a mini-Versailles garden outside.

I turned back to the room and saw bookshelves filled with photos, but not one book. The photos were all of Dun with various other people. One, in particular caught my attention— a young Dun, another gentleman, and a young boy who was Bucky Henderson. Dun wasn't, as Sugar described him, unspectacular. He did have a certain attractiveness that a tall, lean guy sometimes has. He held himself like I remembered Gary Cooper held himself in those old black and white movies. His hair looked thick and tousled, not the unappealing comb-over that he wore today. The boy was unmistakably a young Bucky, with masses of white-blond curls and an eager smile, looking up to the third gentleman, who must have been his father. He was a good-looking man whose casual smile, demeanor, and stance made him seem likeable. I picked the photo up and made my way back to the kitchen.

Tessie had finished washing the dishes and was now polishing the silver sandwich server with pink gunk that was smeared on her apron and all over her fingers.

"Tessie, sorry to bother you again, but I'm just being nosy. Is this Bucky in this photo?"

She bent over to look at the photo I was holding. "Yes, ma'am, Bucky, Dun, and Pappy."

"Who's Pappy?"

"Pappy was Bucky's daddy, but he called him Pappy, and then the rest of us did. Dun and Pappy were partners in the business from the beginning; it was called Wonderson back then, for Wonderly and Henderson."

"What happened to him, to Pappy?"

"One of the saddest days in this town … called Pleasantville back then, was the day Pappy was out jogging and had a heart attack and died at the age of forty-four. Sorrowful day."

"Oh dear, that must have been sad. He looks like a happy guy in the photo."

"Everybody loved Pappy, most of all Bucky and his mom, Georgia."

"Is Georgia still alive?"

"Humph. No she passed a few years later. Story was that old Dun was sniffing around her, gave her some awful disease that she couldn't get rid of and died a young woman at thirty-eight."

"How horrible. Is that true? Could anybody prove it?"

"How can you prove sumpin' like that? Dun was out of bounds for questioning if he was involved or not. Power and money kep' him safe. Until now."

"Did Bucky know this? How old was he?"

"Don't know if Buck knows or not. He was only 'bout ten at the time. How would a kid know 'bout bad stuff like that?"

"So the business was entirely Dun's after that?"

"Not sure how it worked, but I do believe on Dun's decease it goes back to the Hendersons, Bucky that is, but don't know 'bout the details. I hear there's a contract that spells it all out. Sugar'll know."

"Thanks, Tessie. Nice meeting you."

"Ma'am," she acknowledged, now with the pink silver polish on her chin.

My heels clicked against the marble floor and echoed off the walls as I went back to Dun's office to replace the photograph. After I put it back, I pulled out Dun's over-stuffed desk chair and sat down. What was it like to be Dun Wonderly? Where did that wickedness come from? Was he born with it? Did a lack of self-worth motivate him to be on top no matter who he stepped on to get there? Or was it something completely different?

Three heads were bent over the square wood-topped coffee table looking at the Tarot spread. The first card I saw was the *10 of Swords*. You didn't need to be a Tarot card reader to know that didn't look good: a guy face-down with ten swords sticking out of his back. The other one that caught my attention was *The Tower*. I'd had past readings that weren't in the cheery category either. I thought it meant destruction ahead ... or behind? I hoped for Sugar's sake it was for what had already happened. But she still faced a lot of difficulty in the days ahead no matter what. Finding out there was a murderer among her acquaintances was not going to be easy. And not easy for her acquaintances if they found out it was her.

"How's it going?" I asked as the three heads bobbed up to look at me.

"Looks like heavy weather ahead," Sugar sighed.

"*Ten of Swords* most definitely could be Dun's recent unpleasantness," chirped Helen.

Unpleasantness? Is that what she called sweating to death while taking a relaxing steam bath?

"Of course, *The Tower* means destruction, but things *have* been destroyed for you and there might be more. Sometimes a new beginning is just what we need. Don't you agree, Sugar?" questioned Em.

"Yes. Whatever will be, will be. I'm a big girl, I can handle it," Sugar answered wisely.

I hoped so.

To change the subject and because I wanted to know more, I said to Sugar, "I was just talking to Tessie, and she was telling me about Pappy, Bucky's father."

"Oh yes? What did she have to say about dear Pappy?"

"She said he was well loved, died way too young, and that Bucky's mom died a few years later. She didn't say exactly how she died, but that she was also way too young."

"The word in the Flats was that she died from complications of a sexually transmitted disease. People in the Flats know things because most in that community are in service at one of the homes up here "on the hill" as they call it, even though the whole town is as flat as a tire on a bed of nails. But as far as I know that's just conjecture. Could have happened that way with Dun passing on some ghastly disease, but nobody has any proof, and Dun swore on his mother's grave it wasn't true. 'Course, I don't believe a word Dun ever says, said, but it's never been proven."

"Would Bucky know about all of this?"

"Heavens, I can't imagine—him being so young at the time. The only person he'd hear it from would be someone like Tessie, and people loved Bucky so much I can't think they'd tell him news that would hurt him. If anything, they still protect him like he's ten years old," Sugar elaborated, then sank back into the white cushion with a whoosh.

"So the business goes to Bucky now, is that the arrangement?" I continued to dig.

"Yes. Thank goodness. God knows he deserves it with all he's put up with these years. Dun being so rude and brutish to him, and Bucky always taking it with a smile."

"What if Bucky couldn't take over for some reason," I asked.

"Why wouldn't he be able to take over? No reason whatsoever."

"That's at least something," I said.

"I never did read that contract, but I imagine it's pretty straightforward, because Pappy had to sign it, too. Except for "the clause." I read that over and over. Pappy was smart enough to put a clause in to protect the business against Dun's foul ways. That I do remember. I think I can recite it by heart: *Patrick Henderson or Dunbar Wonderly shall not commit any act or do anything which might reasonably be considered to be immoral, deceptive, scandalous, or obscene; or to injure, tarnish, damage or otherwise negatively affect the reputation and goodwill associated with the Company.*"

"Wow."

"Of course, it was to protect Pappy and his family, but if Dun weren't dead, I wouldn't put it past him to turn the tables, and say Pappy, well, now, Bucky, was the one who had to be a good boy. But he is a good boy. Really … the best boy.

"What about Andy, would he have any claim on the business?"

Helen and Em were gathering up the cards, no doubt pretending their daughter wasn't imposing on their charming hostess.

"Andy, good heavens, no. If anything, Dun bought him the farm. The only thing Dun's death would mean to Andy—if that's why you're asking—is to own his farm free and clear. Unless I decided to step in where Dun left off."

I didn't dare ask her what her intentions would be, that would be going a furlong too far.

"I think we'd better be going, Annie, and let Sugar go about her business," Em suggested.

"Yes," Sugar agreed, "and my business right now is to go down to see Denny Earl and ask why he's bothering Ty Patton."

"Why are you so sure Ty didn't have anything to do with Dun's murder? He sure had reason enough." I prodded.

"Of course, I can't be one hundred percent sure, but I've known Ty since he was a pup, and it's just hard to believe," she finished, standing up and smoothing out the wrinkles on her flowered dress.

Thank-you and hugs were evenly distributed between the four of us, and off we went, back to our home away from home.

Not paying close enough attention on the drive to Sugar's I got lost on the way back, and realized we were passing the Flats on our way out of town … and I didn't want to go out of town. There was a tall young black man edging the grass around the entry to the community, and I slowed down,

"Hi, I wonder if you can help me. I'm not sure where we are, and we want to get back to The Dunbar Hotel," I said.

He walked slowly over to the car with what seemed like caution and said, "You want the Dunbar?"

"Yes, I think I'm turned around."

"Well, you're lost, but it's not hard to find your way back." Then he gave expert directions without a hint of a Kentucky accent.

CHAPTER 28

Our chitchat on the way back to the hotel concerned what those Tarot cards might have meant. Em thought there was trouble behind and ahead for Sugar, or at the very least some bumpy days coming. Helen injected some optimism into the reading, meaning it was an end to bad times. "Nothing good can happen without endings," she summed up the reading.

"If you had to guess now from our discussion at Sugar's, who would you put money on to be the murderer?" I questioned.

"We don't bet on death," Helen informed me.

"Can't you ask one of your many ghosts who talk to you who did it?" I pushed on.

"That's not how it works, Annie. You know that. And they're not ghosts, they're spirits; it's an entirely different thing. They might show us a sign that might or might not point us in the right direction, but they would never tell us who did it because, most likely, they don't know either. They're separated from us by a very thin veil, and they're not everyplace at once either, you see," explained Em.

"In my mind, the suspects for Dun's murder, and I hate to say it, are Sugar, Andy Wonderly, Ty Patton, and, probably, Bucky Henderson. Wouldn't you agree?" I submitted.

"That sounds reasonable, but there are quite a few unanswered questions that need to be resolved before a murderer can be named," maintained Em. "Jessica's mother has a motive, as do some of Dun's employees who he treated badly," she continued.

Oh, good grief, I couldn't add any more to my list of people who could be cold-blooded killers. My mind was in overdrive. I needed a lay-down to figure out some of this stuff myself without my Moms' wisdom and metaphysical woohoo. But Em did make sense—there was a whole town of people who Dun could have pissed off enough for them to do him in. Even Tessie.

After hugs at the elevator and a promise to meet at six o'clock to walk down to The Wonder for dinner, my Moms and I went to our separate rooms to rest up for what was to come.

The red light on the phone alerted me I had a message—two as it turned out.

Neil's message: "'Call me now. I need to talk to you."

"Neil? Hey, I got your message. Everything okay? The store hasn't burned down has it?"

"It's not always about the store," he answered.

"Oh? Okay, what's up?"

"I can't go on like this. I can't keep wanting you without any sign that you want me, too. Ya know?"

Of course I knew.

"Wow, this is a serious discussion to have over the phone, don't you think," I answered.

"Maybe, but I needed to say it."

"Okay." But it wasn't okay. My heart sank. What did I expect for God's sake?

"Things can't go on like this."

"Neil, you have to do what's best for you. You should find someone your age that you can make a life with, have a family with," I reasoned.

"Don't tell me what I need. I know what I need, but it doesn't seem like I'm going to get it."

What the hell *was* wrong with me? How could I be in love with a guy twenty years younger, who had no thoughts of a serious career? He had no thought about what would happen if we were to decide to be together for the rest of our lives. And yet, when I was with him I was happy. Was that enough? Is that how it's supposed to be? Where's the manual?

"I'm sorry, Neil, I'm just thinking of your happiness and future."

"That's my responsibility."

"Okay. How do you want to end this conversation?" I said in my adult voice.

"Before you come home, I want you to think about what I said. You have to make a decision—you choose me or I move on."

"Okay." Struggling to think of something meaningful, okay was all that I could come up with.

"That's it?"

"Okay, Neil, I'll give it serious thought. You know how much I care about you, but I'm so conflicted."

"That's your responsibility. You decide what you want to do," he concluded sounding much more adult than I felt.

I wanted to say I love you, because I thought I did; but I was in a contest between my feelings and social mores.

After we hung up, I crashed back into my pillows and cried. Crap. Doesn't this happen to people when they're in their twenties? I couldn't be going through this at my age; it's not right. Then I stopped myself and thought…why isn't it right? I had a lot to think about before I went home, and for the first time I wished it was later instead of sooner.

The second red alert was from Alice Bostick.

"Annie, Ty's home—they let him go. But he would still like to talk to you. Can you call me and set up a time? He doesn't have to live in the cave anymore, since they know he's back in town, but he's still worried about his own safety. Just come to my house. Ty'll be here."

I couldn't call her back. My conversation with Neil was still banging around in my head and heart. I'd nap and call her later.

I dreamed of Pappy. I mean, it was his face, but he was dressed like Vivian in the cream silk dress with black polka dots.

Later, that dream floated in my brain as I let the hot water wash over me in the shower. I sure wished the soothing spray would wash away my conversation with Neil.

"Alice, hi. It's Annie Fillmore."

"Oh, thanks, Annie. Can you come over this evening? Or tomorrow morning?"

"Probably in the morning would be better. My Moms are still here, and we have plans this evening. What did the police say to Ty? Did he share that with you?"

"Just the usual, he said. They don't have any reason to hold him because there's nothing about any of it that connects him except that he was Jess's boyfriend and Mr. Wonderly's employee."

"Okay, I'll see you in the morning about ten, will that work?"

"Perfect. We'll see you then."

I'll see you, but I have nothing to tell you I thought.

CHAPTER 29

The phone rang again—I was starting to feel like Judy Holiday in *The Bells are Ringing*—this time it was Em.

"Annie, dear. We found the bug. But if you think you can hear anything that was said, you'd be incorrect. Somebody might hear from another room, but you wouldn't be able to hear anything. Is that what you thought?"

"Um, yes, I guess I kind of pictured a cassette tape."

"Oh no, dear. It seems it's being transmitted to another location. We'll check your room as well, and room two thirty-seven where you think a murder occurred."

"Where was it in your room?" I asked.

"Behind the headboard. We had to unbolt it from the wall, but we found it."

I should put these two on my payroll—if I had a detective payroll; if I were a detective.

I made reservations for three at The Wonder for six thirty.

While I was fitting my unwilling feet into heels, the phone rang yet again.

It was my rep, Linda, "They found Cal Danvers at the bottom of Pleasant Lake. In his truck. Dead."

"Who's Cal Danvers?"

"Chief Calvin Danvers. Chief of police. Or was until a few weeks ago."

"Oh! The guy Dun said left town about a month before he was supposed to retire. He was going to some land with lakes," I said trying to remember.

"The Land 'tween the Lakes."

"Right. It sounded fishy to me at the time. But that was just after we found out about Jessica, so I guess I wasn't paying close enough attention."

It did sound weird that he would retire without saying good-bye to anybody—especially since he was a life-long resident.

"Jimmy Prescott was out on the lake fishin' when his hook caught something powerful heavy, and it didn't feel right. He called the police, and they found the truck. And Cal. Poor Bucky. That was his uncle."

"Dun said Bucky knew all about the chief retiring…or something like that. I can't recall exactly what he said, but that he was Bucky's relative. What are they saying? Was it an accident?"

"Hard to imagine it was an accident. Cal lived here all his life. Either he drove into the lake, or somebody rolled the truck in. That's what I figure anyway."

"Was he despondent, depressed?" I questioned.

"Not hardly. He was happy-go-lucky. Unless you did something bad. Then he meant business. He always said, 'I always get my man.'"

"The longer I'm here, the worse and worse it gets. Something's rotten in Wonderly. Thanks, Linda. I'm off to dinner with my Moms. Can we talk tomorrow?"

"If I'm not dead."

I hoped she was kidding.

I met the ladies in the lobby at six-fifteen and off we went—not in Wizard of Oz mode this time.

Jeff greeted us at the maître d' stand as we entered. "Good evening, again, Miss Fillmore."

How the heck did he remember me? Had I been misbehaving? Did he remember everybody? Quite the majordomo.

He showed us to a table right next to where Bucky and Vivian Henderson were seated and said, "Alex will be helping you this evening, but please let me know if you need anything else."

Once we were seated, I realized I had to say something about Bucky's uncle. But what was he doing having a romantic dinner with his wife on a night when there was such terrible news about his own uncle. Also he looked like he was dressed to celebrate, not to mourn, and way different than I had noticed before. This evening he was in a black silk shirt and some form-fitting jeans.

I got up to greet them at their table. "Hi, Bucky. Hi, Vivian. I'm so sorry about your uncle, Bucky."

He hesitated for a moment, maybe less, then said, "We were just talking about good old Cal. We loved him so much. Everybody did. This is quite a shock, especially after losing Dun."

He lowered his head somberly.

"At one of our luncheons Dun said you knew all about Cal retiring to Land 'tween the Lakes," I stated.

He looked over at Vivian, who almost imperceptibly nodded for him to proceed.

"Dun. He didn't know what he was talking about. Cal and I were related, but we aren't close. Weren't close. He's a character. We loved him, but he lived his own life and made clear he didn't want any interference. And we respected his wishes. I had no idea he was retiring, and shocked like everybody else when he didn't even say good-bye. And even more shocked when they found him at the bottom of the lake."

"As an outsider, I have to say, there have been a lot of dead bodies in Wonderly since I arrived on Friday."

"That's the last thing we want our guests to think about this town. We've always been a happy place. This has just been an unfortunate run of trouble. Some ill wind blew in, and we dearly hope it's over," he said, head down, looking pretty miserable.

Was I the ill wind that blew in? I sure hoped not.

"I hope it's over too. And I hope I can go home to *my* happy place. Very soon." I added.

"On a lighter note, I hope you have received our invitation for a tour of the Wonderly Distillery?"

"No, Bucky, I haven't received an invitation."

I realized he hadn't met Helen and Em. "Please let me introduce you to my Moms."

He stood up, walked over to our table, and turned to Vivian, "Viv, come say hello to Annie's family."

After introductions, I said, "I haven't received any invitations. How would it have been delivered?"

"Should have been slipped under your door this evening," Bucky answered.

"Perhaps it will be there when we get back to the hotel," I said hopefully.

"Well, if not, consider this an invitation. Tomorrow evening at six. We'll be there to greet you. And I hope these lovely ladies will join you," Bucky said.

"That should be fun. I've been wanting to have a tour, and now we can all go. What do you think?" I asked my Moms.

"A distillery, how interesting. I'd very much like to see the fermentation process," agreed Em.

Once they left the table and we settled in to order our drinks from Alex, I looked up to see Andy Wonderly at the bar. I excused myself again from the table and went to meet him.

"Andy, hi. Annie Fillmore." Who knew if he remembered my name?

"Good evening, welcome to The Wonder," he said graciously, "and your lovely mothers," he added, nodding in their direction.

Ungraciously, I said, "Andy, I know Dun didn't drive you home the other night when you were in his office as you said. I was there."

"There? You were in Dun's office?" he asked, smirking.

"I was doing some work at one of the cubes, and I heard you and Dun, and you left before he did, so he didn't drive you home. I haven't mentioned this to the police, but you might want to tell me what your car was doing outside the warehouse this morning so I don't have to pass it on to them."

"Well now. One moment," he said as he leaned over toward the bartender. "Put table twelve's drinks on my tab, Don, and please send a bottle of our best champagne as well."

"That's totally unnecessary, Andy."

"It's my pleasure. I do this for all my special guests."

"So about your car being parked outside the warehouse that morning?"

"Actually it had been parked there a few days. When I came in to talk to Dun, I parked in the back as usual, but when I came out, she wouldn't start and the dang thing is practically new. It was too late to call Dandy, so I walked back to the hotel and called a cab—a helluva inconvenience. When

Dandy finally picked her up, he tells me that she'd been tampered with. What the hell? Pardon my language, ma'am."

"My goodness. What was done to it?"

"Said they took one of the plugs, spark plugs. Well, then I wanted him to go over it tooth and nail to make sure nothing else was fiddled with. And so he did, and all was dandy, heh heh. Who the hell would take my spark plug, and why?"

Who and why indeed?

"But your car's been there since Sunday. Why didn't you get it checked out sooner?"

"You obviously don't own a horse farm. With so much to do, my cars aren't the first thing I think of, and I didn't think of it until yesterday. I know, I know, I'm a ding-a-ling."

If he was telling the truth, who would steal his spark plug and why? A lot of questions hung in the bar air along with the sound of clinking glasses.

It seemed the more I knew, the more unanswered questions there were. Maybe this is how life works. Could be that old saw "what you don't know won't hurt you" has a ring of truth to it?

"I'm sorry," I said to Helen and Em when I returned to the table. "I wanted to ask Andy why his car was parked outside the warehouse the other night. He said it had been there for a few nights and someone had tampered with it."

"It is hard to believe a lovely gentleman like Andy would be involved in something as sordid as his brother's murder," Em cajoled.

"Now, Mom, don't let your personal feelings interfere with our investigation."

"Those aren't my *personal* feelings, Annie," she said, and I swear she blushed.

I dropped the topic as quick as Thelma and Louise drove off that cliff. I never wanted to make them feel embarrassed or foolish.

We enjoyed our fancy dinner with lots of appreciation from Helen and Em. As much as I was enjoying the seared sea scallops and basil corn, my mind was on Andy's car and who would have taken his spark plug and why. And why was it really parked there that long? I could understand stealing the car, but a spark plug?

Andy's champagne arrived at our table in an ice bucket. After my Scotch and both the ladies' drinks, the bubbly would have been way too much. But not wanting to hurt Andy's feelings we each allowed ourselves a few sips. Okay, I drank a glass. At which point I noticed him standing by my chair. "Oh, Andy, thanks again for the champagne, but I don't think we can enjoy it all."

"No problem, let's send the rest over to Bucky and Vivian to celebrate. I guess Bucky will be taking over Wonderly Entertainment now."

I didn't say a word.

"Yes, Andy, that's so thoughtful of you," chimed in Em. "Helen and I are leaving Friday, but we're happy to have the chance to say good-bye and to thank you for your hospitality. It's been a memorable visit to Kentucky."

"Leaving? You're leaving?" I barked.

"Yes, darling. We didn't want to upset you, but we must get back. We have so much on our agenda. We *were* going to tell you when we said good night," Helen murmured.

"Are you flying out of Lou'ville?" Andy asked.

"We flew into Louisville on the way here, then took a little puddle jumper not far from here. But I suppose we could have just taken a taxi from Louisville to Wonderly—perhaps we'll do that Friday," Em said.

"I'll hear none of it. What time is your flight?" questioned Andy.

"The flight from Louisville leaves at five-thirty and arrives at LaGuardia a little after seven-thirty," Helen said fumbling in her purse for the exact time.

"In the mornin'? Five-thirty a.m.?" asked Andy.

"No dear, in the evening, so, really, we do have one full day," declared Em.

"I'll drive you ladies to Lou'ville. You'll be much more comfortable in my Cadillac than you will in that puddle jumper. Was it Jumpin' Jimmy?"

"I believe that is what he called himself," Helen remembered.

"Good Lord, no way I'm going to let him take precious cargo like you, two times. I insist upon picking you up and personally delivering you to L.I.A."

Precious cargo? Was this guy for real?

"L.I.A?" questioned Helen.

"Lou'ville International Airport," he said. "Why don't we go early, have lunch, and take a tour of some of the historic homes in Lou'ville before your flight. I believe you'll find that a delightful way to spend your last day in Kentucky," submitted Andy.

"You are kind indeed," Em chirped, "a perfect example of a Kentucky gentleman."

Unless he was a murderer. Can a murderer also be a gentleman?

They both looked at me with apology in their eyes. I knew they wanted to spend the day with Andy and tour Louisville, especially the old homes, thinking about antebellum women. Maybe even talking to one or two of their spirits…or ghosts. Whichever happened to be hanging around.

"Of course you have to do that, what a great way to end your visit," I said, keeping a stiff upper lip.

As Bucky said, there was an invitation slipped under my door for a tour of the Bourbon Distillery the next day. That should be fun I thought.

I was not becoming accustomed to the hotel bed, and I tossed and turned with now possibly four murders chugging around in my brain, circling like a toy train on a track.

Maybe Ty Patton would come up with more concrete information than what he said Jessica told him— "I guess what Bobby Crane said is true." What did Bobby Crane tell her that she thought was true? If I knew that, I'd be a lot closer to going home. That is, if I really wanted to go home in light of Neil's latest phone call.

CHAPTER 30

Helen and Em had risen at their normal time and were in my room to see if they could search for the bug—although what good would it do without being able to listen to it? I never underestimated them though. I would love to have known the conversations in room 237 on October 10 and October 11. If they could have unearthed that, I would be going home.

I left my Moms unbolting the headboards and drove over to Alice's. I wondered in earnest how long I could conceivably stay in Wonderly, not making the daily decisions for Annie's.

I sometimes felt like a symphony conductor when it came to my store. But come to think of it, did an orchestra really need a conductor at all, or are they just for show? Either way, they had their purpose. What hubris, comparing myself to Lenny Bernstein.

Ty was standing on Alice's front porch when I pulled into her driveway, arms folded across his chest and looking like a guy modelling jeans. His hair needed a good cut...but, hey.

"Can we take a walk?" he asked as I strolled across the grass toward him.

"Sure."

Heading toward the lake, I was hoping he wouldn't drag me into the pump house again, but he stopped a few paces from the beach, and we sat on some boulders that fronted the woods that may have led to his cave.

"So, what did the police have to say?"

"Pretty much what you'd expect. Where was I when both Jessica and Dun were murdered? They haven't actually accepted one hundred percent that Jess was murdered, but I have. And I let them know that."

"Did you tell them Jessica said, 'I guess what Bobby Crane said is true.'?"

"No. Because I don't know what that is, and it might look like I'm just deflecting suspicion away from me, ya know."

"Is there any way we can figure out what Jessica meant? You knew her best, knew how she thought. Do you even have a guess at what that could be?"

"Jess didn't think rationally most of the time. She had a huge heart and was kind to everybody, but she lived a pie-in-the-sky kind of existence. If she wanted something, she thought she would get it, like going to Hollywood and being another Marilyn Monroe. If she thought a rumor was going to get her closer to that goal, she wouldn't even question if it were true or not. So there's no way of knowing if Bobby told her a lie just to get her in bed, or if he was telling her something that was true. The two people who know that are dead."

"Alice said you were concerned about your safety, too."

"Well, yeah. If whatever Jess knew was true, whoever killed her might think I know that secret, too."

"Are you staying at your house with your dad?"

"No. I'm looking in on him, making sure he hasn't fallen down the stairs, if he can even get up the stairs. Alice has been doing that for me while I've been hiding out, but he's my responsibility. I can't stay there safely until this mess is settled."

"Of course. Just be very careful. It seems we have a killer out there who may not be done."

"I'm not a fool, I'll be extra careful. I just wanted to know if you know something I don't."

"Not a thing, I'm afraid. I have a few loose ends I'd like to tie up. At this point those loose ends don't amount to much. But I have to get back to my store in Briartown, so I'm going to be concentrating on getting to the bottom of this if the police don't do it soon."

"I wouldn't get my hopes up on the police doing anything. From my conversation with them, they seem clueless."

And that was that. We walked back to my car, and I returned to the hotel to see what Helen and Em were up to.

When I returned from my meeting with Ty, Daisy and Hermy were sitting in the lobby surrounded by their suitcases.

"You're still here," I said. "I haven't seen you in a few days."

"Oh, we've been off having fun in Louisville and Lexington, but I think we're about done. Of course, we're going to miss the special tour of the distillery this evening, but we've been through it two times now, so that's probably enough—even though this time it would be with the new president," she sighed.

"You waiting for a cab?" I asked.

"No, we're waiting for our videos. We made a huge order because the prices were so low." Then she whispered, "Of course, because we're such good customers and we order so much, we even got a better deal. Most people don't order like us unless they're Blockbuster," she said and winked.

Good gravy. (As Helen would say.)

"Toot toot, coming through," said Linda pushing a large cart of videos for Video Vixen's lucky customers.

"Hey, don't go away," Linda said to me, "I have to get another cart, and I'm bringing you something, too."

Daisy, Hermy, and I made small talk until Linda was back with another full cart and a small package for me. Maybe another episode of Bare Bottom Babes, I thought.

Linda handed me the package and said, "This is the video Jessica had in her hand when she died. Not the exact video but the same title. Why? I have no idea."

The Dixons and I said our good-byes with promises to be in touch when we got back to the Cincinnati area.

I headed back to my room to look at the video.

Helen and Em were still in my room, with the adjoining door to room 237 wide open. "We found the bug in your room, dear," Em announced. The headboard was sitting in the middle of the room with screwdrivers and a hammer. "We won't dismantle the headboard in room two thirty-seven. What would be the sense in that if we couldn't hear anything anyway?"

Always so sensible.

We had the afternoon to while away, but my Moms decided they wanted to pack, meditate, and "make contact."

Given their unavailability, I decided to make contact with my pillow.

CHAPTER 31

The rickety wooden steps to the front of the grey clapboard building didn't match the elaborate gold lettered sign over the door, WONDERLY BOURBON DISTILLERY, which was fashioned in the same art deco lettering as the invitations. Actually, the lettering was what Dun used on every sign.

Once inside, we saw Bucky and Vivian standing in front of a huge photograph of Dun and greeting their guests. I had noticed Bucky was maybe five nine, but I hadn't noticed he was shorter than Vivian. I checked out her shoes to gauge how tall she might have been without the heels. This is something I know about, since I'm always trying to elevate my five feet two. My seat-of-the-pants guess was she was about his same height, maybe a hair and a half taller. Bucky was, as the night before, wearing those excellent jeans and a Harris Tweed jacket over a black T-shirt—so different from his work mufti. His hair was different, too. It was now in the popular styled Caesar haircut instead of the hair parted do that he had been sporting. And no eyeglasses.

Vivian matched his sophistication in a black pantsuit with a tie waist. She added a pair of cream-colored leather gloves with no fingers. I thought it was a bit over the top for the occasion, but she did look first-class.

Once we were all assembled—I counted thirteen people—Bucky said a few words.

"Greetings and welcome to Wonderly Distillery, home of some of the world's finest bourbon. I'm Bucky Henderson and this is my wife, Vivian." She bowed her head in recognition. "I'm going to turn over the tour to Andrew Buddingsly, who's been working in this distillery for close on to twenty-four years. He's as old as some of our bourbon. So without further ado, Andrew, take it away."

"Howdy. Glad you could join us this evening for a tour of one of the best small batch distilleries in Kentucky, or at least *I* think it's one of the best."

I nudged Em, and she gave me "the look." The look meant, behave yourself.

Andrew went on, "We have a special natural resource here in Kentucky, and it's something you should remember, limestone. Limestone you ask. Why? Because the bourbon you will taste at the end of this tour, in fact all of the bourbon produced in the great Commonwealth of Kentucky, owes its taste to limestone. All the water used in the making of bourbon filters through limestone, and when it does it picks up a sweet flavor of calcium, while it removes iron that would make the end product taste bitter instead of smooth. Our water comes from the crick that runs back of this here distillery."

"So *all* the water in Kentucky bourbon is filtered through limestone?" asked a tourist in the back.

"Yes sir," retorted Andrew. "Now let me take you on a tour. A tour that starts out with corn and ends up with a night on the town.

Andrew walked up a few creaky steps, took a left through one room and then a right, into a room with huge metal containers.

"These here are the grinders. All bourbon by law has to be fifty-one percent corn, and these grinders do a job on that corn releasing the starch. In other batches the machine grinds up malted barley and rye. Here at Wonderly we use 'bout seventy percent corn."

"So in the end, bourbon consists of all of those grains. Corn, barley, and rye?" someone asked.

"Yes, sir, you got that right. Well, some distilleries use wheat instead of rye, but here at Wonderly, we use rye."

"After the grinding, we cook the corn, barley, and rye with the limestone water; then we add our special yeast formulation, and the grain becomes mash."

"Is there a difference between mash and sour mash?" asked Em.

"Yes, ma'am. Great question. Bourbon is aged at least two years in charred oak barrels. But I'm getting ahead of myself a bit. The sour mash whiskey uses the same bourbon recipe, but it starts the process from a previous batch of mash, kinda like sourdough starter for bread. The end product of sour mash has a sweet flavor. Wonderly Bourbon is sour mash.

Follow me, and we'll take a look at the cypress wood tubs where the fermentation takes place."

We followed Andrew down a few steps, around a bend, and up a few more steps to a room with five huge tubs. The floors creaked as we made our way from room to room, and I wondered if they were reinforced to hold the weight, not only of the grinders and tubs, but of all the visitors as well. The place looked like a big brother to Dandy's garage, holding on by a thread.

"Now these here are the tubs where the yeast is added, and what you see here in the tubs is the different stages of fermentation. Once the yeast works its magic, the mash becomes a bubbling brew that any witch would envy. The bubbling you see is the release of carbon dioxide gas as the sugars in the grain ferment and become alcohol, kind of a sour beer. Whoopee.

"Now down to the place where the alcohol leaves the waste."

That room had beautiful onion-shaped copper pot stills into which that sour beer is fed apparently.

"Then more magic," Andrew reported. "The alcohol separates from the wash as the alcohol vapor rises into pipes surrounded by cold water tubes. Bam, that vapor now condenses into liquid again and is now alcohol that's about one hundred and twenty-five proof. After it's distilled one more time into a doubler, the alcohol comes out at about one hundred and thirty-five proof. And clean."

Andrew called the purified alcohol Low Wine. I'm pretty sure that was also known as white lightening.

He continued explaining that the Low Wine is poured into charred oak barrels and stored for up to twenty-three years, which gives bourbon its color and flavor. He said changes in the atmosphere in the storage facility force the liquid in and out of the charred wood. Or at least I think that's what he said. He added more, but I had listened enough and was ready for what he had called "a night on the town."

Four round tables set for four each were set up on a deck off the back of the building. At each place were two tiny decanters of bourbon and a side plate of chocolate. The decanters, Andrew said, held different vintages of bourbon.

Once we were seated we enjoyed the view overlooking a creek, and, in the far distance, rolling Kentucky hills. Bourbon with a view.

Helen, Em, and I sat at a table alone. Others sat with people they seemed to know. Although Bucky and Vivian weren't on the tour with us, they sat at one of the other tables but weren't sampling what they now, probably, owned. How was that going to work? So many questions about who would be endowed with Dun's riches.

"Did you see Vivian is wearing the same kind of gloves with the fingers cut off that she wore last night at dinner? Last night the gloves were black," noticed Helen.

"You know, I didn't notice her gloves last night," I replied. Was she wearing those kind of gloves the first night I met her at Dun's party? I don't think so, because I did notice her strong hands and legs that evening, and what a beautiful contrast they made to her exquisite face. Those gloves were quite a fashion statement anywhere, but especially in a small town like Wonderly.

After we all had enjoyed our bourbon and chocolate, Andrew led us back through the maze of rooms to the entrance, where we said good night. Bucky and Vivian weren't among the group for us to bestow our thanks.

I bid farewell to my Moms in their room in case I missed them in the morning. They'd be getting up and having breakfast early. Andy was picking them up at nine thirty, so there was a good chance this would be the last time I saw them in Kentucky. Our eyes were all moist with our final hug, but I was happy they were going to see Louisville before they went home.

Once back in my room I saw the boxed video Linda had given me that I had thrown on the bed. What the heck, it was only nine thirty—maybe I'd see why Jessica had this video in her hand when she was killed.

Pretty Woman? What would this movie have to do with Jessica's death? Jessica was a pretty woman, sure, but aside from that I was puzzled. I slipped the video into the VCR player and waited, holding my breath.

In the opening scene Jason Alexander is at a party with Richard Gere. Then Gere leaves the party in Jason Alexander's car.

The next shots are dark, and I couldn't really hear what the actors were saying until the part where Richard Gere pulls up his car looking for directions. Julia Roberts gets in and introduces herself. At three minutes and fifty-two seconds into the video, I knew who Jessica's murderer was. "Oh, my God," I screamed to the empty room.

Laying on the bed and going over what I knew, everything came together—the entire puzzle. There were still holes that needed filling in, and lots of questions, but I knew who the murderer was, and first thing the next morning I was going to see Chief Earl to let him know I had solved the murder. I was going back to Briartown, maybe as early as Friday night.

But what was I going to tell Neil?

Five hours sleep is not nearly enough for someone who needs eight hours to function. But that's all I got that night. The next day turned out to be one where it would have been extremely helpful if I had had the acuity of Hercule Poirot and the agility of James Bond.

CHAPTER 32

Even before I'd had a sip of my morning coffee I called Chief Earl.

"Wonderly Police Department, how can I help?" Amanda answered.

"Hi Amanda, this is Annie Fillmore. I was in on Sunday to have my fingerprints taken. I'd like to see Chief Earl this morning."

"The reason for your visit to see the chief?"

"I believe I know who killed Jessica Bostick, Dun Wonderly, and Bobby Crane, and, maybe, Cal Danvers."

"Bobby Crane, who's he?" she asked.

"Please let me know the soonest I can see Chief Earl," I insisted.

"Hold on," she said with an exasperated sigh.

"Denny Earl," was the next voice I heard.

"Good morning, Chief Earl, this is Annie Fillmore, and…"

"Ya, got it. What's this about you know who killed Jessica and Dun, and," he snorted, "Bobby Crane?"

"I believe I have valid information to tie the three murders together. May I come see you this morning?"

"Well I guess I can't turn away Mrs. Columbo," snort, snort. "How 'bout you get here about one o'clock." That's Ms. Columbo!

"I'll be there. Thank you." That's not at all what I wanted to say, but I wanted him to listen to me, so I swallowed the snide words.

Dressed and antsy, I went down to have breakfast, hopefully, for the last time at The Dunbar Hotel.

Linda was walking across the lobby toward the offices with a cup of coffee, "Linda, hey, thank you for the *Pretty Woman* video."

"Did it help?" she asked.

"Yes, I think I know who the murderer is." The second that was out of my mouth I knew I shouldn't have said it. For God's sake, I *should* be more like Columbo. "But you absolutely cannot tell anybody that I might have a suspect. Please promise me."

"Scout's honor," she said, shuffling off to sell videos.

That was a big mistake, BIG, as Julia Roberts tells the snooty clerks in the movie, *Pretty Woman.* Slightly different circumstances, but the results could be deadly.

After breakfast, with the greatest of optimism, I packed what I came with along with the paraphernalia I was gifted by the studios, Marilyn, and my Moms. Daisy Dixon was right, I did need another suitcase. Instead I packed the rest of it in plastic bags that had accumulated over the week.

Gearing up for my meeting with Chief Earl, I wrote a list of everything I wanted to say and my reasoning behind it, like I do when I go to my doctor. Without a list to rely on I usually answer his question about what's bothering me with "Nothing, I'm fine."

I was pacing and fidgeting, so I took a walk to town and back to burn off some nervous energy. It was about twelve thirty when I decided to drive over to Placid Street, feeling anything but. I got there around twelve forty and waited in my car. Being in that parking spot reminded me of Neil, which reminded me I had to decide what to say to him. But how much can a woman think about in one day? My head was about to explode.

"So what has the great street detective come up with that I can't?" Denny Earl said to me as I was sitting opposite him in his office.

When he put it that way.

"Did you take the opportunity to look at the *Pretty Woman* video that Jessica was holding when she was murdered?" I asked.

"I didn't personally, but I guess one of the detectives took a look. If they found anything they would have shared that with me first thing. So you're inferring that *you* found something on that tape that would tell us who murdered two people? Three in your opinion?"

I read from my list of how and why Bobby Crane, Jessica Bostick, Dun Wonderly, and possibly Chief Danvers were killed, and by whom. And the real clincher, I thought, was that I had in my possession Bucky Henderson's contact lens that must have come loose from his eye in room 237.

He looked at me for a few seconds before belching out a guffaw that almost blew me across the room. "You know lady, you are one mixed-up person. We know these people down here. You've been here for what, a week, and you think you can determine what makes everybody tick? You have guts, I'll give you that. Here's a piece of good news though. Go home. Leave us be. We'll figure this out on our own. You are now free to leave Wonderly, you've done enough damage."

What else was there to say? Could I go back to Briartown knowing who murdered three people and just let it go? I didn't think so.

I knew exactly what I had to do when I got back to the hotel—call Cincinnati detective Tom Ward. Tom and I had collaborated to solve a crime the previous year. He'd understand.

"Get the hell out of there today. Leave it alone. All murders aren't solved, and maybe these three or four won't be either," was the unwanted response from Tom, whom I considered my friend. Then he added, "I'll do what I can, but you get out of that town."

"But, but..."

"No buts, Annie. Come home now."

"Okay, okay," I conceded, sounding like I was fourteen instead of the adult some people thought I was.

Perhaps a last ditch effort, but worth a try, "Alice, it's Annie Fillmore. Is Ty around, or can I find him in the next hour or so?"

"He's out back, would you like to talk to him?"

"May I come over? I need to speak with him."

I don't know why I expected Ty to help me bring the murderer to justice, but I trusted him for some reason, call it an honest vibe I got from him. And he wanted Jessica's killer to be caught as much as I did. Even more so.

Again, Ty was waiting for me on the porch in his GQ stance, but I wanted more than pulchritude from him. I needed inside information.

We walked to the same boulders as we had sat on before. Then I asked him a question that was difficult to ask.

"Ty, I don't know a proper way to ask this, so I'm just going to spit it out. But let me say first that it has everything to do with finding out who killed Jessica, okay?"

"I can take it," he said.

"When you were having sex with Bucky, sorry, did you get the impression that was the first time he had ever had homosexual sex? I don't know if that's the right terminology, but you get it, right?

"Oh yeah, I get it. Umm, it was so disgusting to me I tried not to think about anything but getting it over with and getting the money."

"If that's all you can tell me, let me tell you what I found."

And for the next fifteen minutes or so I told him my theory and how I think it all happened

He was aghast at first, but the more we talked it over, the more he agreed that's pretty much how it must have happened ... with all three murders. For some reason Bobby Crane wasn't even being acknowledged to be dead, no less murdered. So really, four murders if you count Cal Danvers. And, of course, I did.

What we couldn't decide was how to go forward if Chief Earl wasn't taking me seriously. All I knew was that I was going home to Ohio, if not that night, then definitely the next morning. We decided to go our separate ways and come up with a plan to trap the killer, if not now, some day.

CHAPTER 33

Fatigued and anxious doesn't make a great combo, but that's what I was when I walked into room 239.

A printed invitation card had been slid under the door and was awaiting me.

WONDERLY DISTILLERY

INVITES YOU TO A PRE-DINNER EVENING ON OUR DECK

TO SAMPLE SOME OF OUR FINEST BOURBONS, ACCOMPANIED BY LOCAL CHEESES AND DELICACIES.

6 P.M. FRIDAY, OCTOBER 25

A hand-written note at the bottom of the invitation said "for locals and special guests only".

That was an invitation I was going to accept, but a nap was in order so I wouldn't be slobbering over the bourbon. How many naps had I taken in Wonderly? Was the town a soporific, or was I exhausted from being overly involved in everybody else's business?

After I awoke, I put on my black dress, slipped into my heels, and threw on my blue sweater because there might be a chill in the air as there was the previous evening.

Half-way out the door I remembered I had never returned the scissors that helped me unearth the aroma of the Glade Country Air Freshener, so I went back in, tucked them in my pocket, and was off to sample some bourbon, and maybe to catch a murderer.

Perhaps I should have been more on edge at the thought of coming face to face with a killer, but I figured there'd be enough people at the bourbon sipping to cover me.

The fact that there were no cars in the parking lot didn't seem odd since it was a local affair. My watch said six-fifteen, so maybe everybody was already on the deck; I heard music coming from somewhere. How the heck did we get to the back deck? I couldn't remember because there were so many twists and turns. I started out in the grinder room, and then somehow got to the distiller room with the copper pot stills, then to the fermentations tubs. But I still couldn't find my way to the back. Shouldn't they have thought to put arrows?

While I was standing in front of one of the bubbling tubs of witch's brew trying to figure out how to get to the outside deck, Vivian Henderson appeared from one of the other rooms.

"Hi, Vivian, I'm trying to find the deck for the bourbon tasting."

"You've come to the right place," she answered.

"Huh?"

"Word on the street is you know who killed Jessica, Dun, and Bobby, is that right?"

Word on the street? Linda opened her big mouth.

"Uh."

Why couldn't I think of something pithy to say like Sam Spade would say in a tight spot?

I gathered myself. "Do you know who killed them, Vivian?"

"No, I don't know and neither does Chief Denny, so why are people saying *you* know?"

"I'm sure you're familiar with the District Seven law, right?" What the hell was I saying?

"District Seven?" she asked.

"Right, when a murder that occurs in one district hasn't been resolved, districts in seven surrounding towns or counties have the right and obligation to step in and attempt to solve those crimes. I know people in two of those districts," I lied. "And I've passed on what I know to those two districts since Chief Earl doesn't believe me." I may not be pithy but I'm always quick to lie like a rug.

"You're full of shit," she said, so unladylike, but then she wasn't exactly a lady. Especially with the rod she produced in her right hand.

"So Vivian, are you a he or a she?" I asked, clearly guessing at what her gender was.

"I'm both, if you must know, but I've known I was a female since about the age I started remembering stuff … I knew I was different. But now that Dun's dead I'm having the full reassignment surgery. "

"Why all the murder? You and Bucky could have had a beautiful life if not for that," I pleaded.

"We're going to have a beautiful life *because* of the murders. That awful excuse for a human being, Bobby Crane, had to go. He was going to either blackmail us for the rest of our lives about me being born male, or he was going to out us. Neither one was an option."

"But Vivian, the world is changing, people would have accepted you as you are."

"In Wonderly, Kentucky? Dunbar Wonderly... ha. You haven't been here long enough to understand this town is still in the dark ages. And that stupid little idiot, Jessica Bostick. Boy I hated to do that to her, but she was going to blackmail me since Bobby Crane told her about me to get her in bed with him. He was the scum of the earth."

Murdering three people may not be considered cream off the top.

"What happened to Bobby? Nobody seems to know." I asked casually. I may have sounded nonchalant, but my body was clenched like a fist.

"He met the same end you're going to meet. Somebody sipping fine bourbon or a not so fine bourbon will be sipping a bit of you and Bobby," she said, gesturing with her hand that didn't have the gun in it toward the bubbling mash.

"Is Bucky in on this? Does he know what you've done?" I asked as blithely as possible for someone who's about to be macerated in a batch of hooch.

"Are you crazy? Of course he knows. He knows that he's acted like a buffoon for twenty odd years to make Dun think he was a moron. Ya know Dun had no intention of ever letting Wonderly Enterprises go to Bucky, no matter what the contract between Dun and Pappy said. Dun wants Wonderly Entertainment to stay in the family. That thought has been cooking in Dun's sick mind ever since he signed the agreement; even more after Pappy died."

I started inching my way as slowly as I could around the tub, thinking I could at least forestall being killed if she shot a hole in the tub instead of in me.

"Is that why Dun came up with the scheme for Ty Patton to have sex with Bucky? I know about the clause in the contract that Dun and Pappy signed."

"Aren't you a smarty pants, but you'll have to ask Dun when you meet him, ha ha. You are spot on."

"So you killed Dun, too, so Bucky could be the rightful heir to Wonderly Enterprises?"

"It's not like I didn't warn Dun to back off. I met up with him several times to tell him to let it go or there'd be consequences. I told him for the last time when I interrupted one of his midnight swims. But, sad for him, he didn't take me seriously."

By this time I'd moved around the side of the tub, slinking closer to the back, where I might have some cover.

"I killed Dun because he was the worst son of a bitch I'd ever met. He'd screw a hole in the wall if nobody was looking. He was rotten to everybody who couldn't earn him a buck, or couldn't do him a favor. I don't know how Sugar refrained from stabbing him in his sleep from so much shagging around all those years. She's a saint."

"One last question … was that Bucky's contact lens I found in room two thirty-seven?"

"Hey, stopping talking, you don't need to know anything when you're dead.

She clearly didn't know my mothers.

"If I'm going to die anyway, at least let me go with some answers," I begged.

"Okay, last one," she acceded.

"Was that you in my room the night I hit someone next to my bed?"

"Yep, guilty. I needed to find Bucky's damn contact lens, and I figured with what I'd heard about you, you might have had it."

"And what about Andy's spark plug. Did you take that?"

"We figured Andy would have been the most likely murder suspect especially since his car was outside the warehouse the morning after Dun showed up dead. Pretty clever, huh?"

"Not clever enough, Vivian. The police know his car had been there for a few days. And those gloves aren't a fashion statement are they? They're to cover up the slashes on your hands from the splinters in the long rifle you shoved in the door to lock Dun in the steam room." I spit it out quickly because, really, that was two questions.

"Enough. Now you're annoying me, and it's going to be much easier to get rid of you," she said lifting the revolver to take closer aim.

I ducked behind the tub, flipped on my back, and did a backward soldier crawl moving toward the next bubbling batch. If she was going to shoot me, I wanted to see her face. The only weapon I had was in my pocket. I grabbed the scissors. As soon as she was next to me, aiming that damn gun at my head, I slammed the scissors into her calf as hard as I could. She screamed and doubled over as I got to my feet and attempted to get the gun out of her hand. We were battling for it when she bent me over backward toward the yeasty tub of mash. She was strong, much stronger than I was, probably because she had male muscles even if she looked like a stunning woman. I bit her arm that was closest to me, she screamed again but persisted. I could feel my hair cooking in that brew and it felt like my back was about to break.

"Unhand her now or I'll shoot to kill."

I knew who that voice belonged to. But Em was supposed to be winging her way back East. What was going on?

"Wait, you're this one's mother, right?"

"Unhand her now," Em bellowed again. Even in this horrifying scenario, I thought, unhand her? It sounded like I was bound to railroad tracks by a villain with a handlebar moustache. I love that woman.

Em took a shot so close to Vivian's head I could see her red bob move as if by a slight breeze. Did Em miss, or was this a warning shot?

Vivian's hold on me slackened for a moment, and I wrenched away from her like a mouse darting away from a cat. Thank God I didn't have a tail for her to step on.

Another voice emerged from behind me from a door I hadn't noticed, "Vivian and I will be leaving now; we'll be taking this woman with us to make sure we're not followed."

This woman? Me?

"You seem like a nice old woman," he said to Em, "but if you don't leave by these stairs right now, I'll shoot your daughter, or whoever she is to you."

Em stretched herself up to her full height with a formidable hauteur, and looked at me.

"Go ahead, Mom. Please," I begged.

She did, but reluctantly I could tell.

Bucky backed into the door he had come from, dragging me, because I wasn't going along willingly. That gun in his hand was a pretty good deterrent to my fleeing.

He pulled me down about five winding wooden steps through a door to the outside under the deck. They both had guns, but Vivian seemed to be in too much pain from her leg wound to shoot straight. I wasn't going voluntarily though. This crazy duo had killed four people, what was a fifth to them? Except maybe a bottle of their vintage bourbon.

My left shoe had come off from all the dragging, and without thinking, as Bucky momentarily was seeing to Vivian's leg, I whacked him in the groin with it. He doubled over and I gave him another kick with my right foot. Then I ran as fast as I could. I felt a bullet whiz by my head, and I started to serpentine. What was that movie with the serpentine scene?

Finally getting to the edge of the back wall of the distillery, I was about to turn the corner when Bucky grabbed me again; but he was still panting hard, so I elbowed him in the stomach. That probably wasn't as effective as was Chief Denny Earl coming toward us with gun in hand.

"Buck, oh Bucky, why did you do this to yourself? You had it all," the chief groaned.

Do this to *himself?* What about the four cadavers?

When I walked a little farther around the building, there were Em and Helen standing with open arms.

"Why are you here? Didn't you go to Louisville with Andy this morning?" I asked.

"Yes, Annie. We went, but when we were touring the Conrad-Caldwell home, we both knew we had to return to you. We sensed that you were in dire trouble," Em informed me.

"Did one of the house ghosts tell you?" I asked, half kidding.

"We just know, dear, no need for meddlesome ghosts," Helen explained.

"Come along," Annie, "we're through here. Let's get you a shot of whiskey to settle your nerves. You may not think you're a wreck, but you will be," predicted Em as she led me to Andy's car.

"You're driving Andy's Cadillac?" I asked stupidly, because Em was behind the wheel.

"Yes, there was no need for him to get involved in anything so dangerous. He's a gentle soul, unlike his brother."

Back in room 239, they propped me up on the pillows, ordered a Scotch from the bar, and sat on either side of me, holding my hands.

"*The In-Laws*," I remembered.

"What, dear, are you okay, are you hallucinating?" asked Helen.

"No, that's the name of the movie with 'serpentine' I was trying to think of as I was running away from Bucky."

"Bring the Scotch, Em; Annie is having a problem reorienting."

"I'm fine, Mom, just a little shaky."

"You were very brave, Annie," complimented Helen.

"If quite foolish to be taking on more than you could handle," cajoled Em. "We were so grateful to have found that fake invitation on the desk in your room. Even more grateful that your friend from Cincinnati, that lovely Detective Ward, called down to Wonderly to ask the chief of police to follow you to make sure you didn't do anything dangerous before you left town."

What possesses me to do these kinds of things? I didn't ask my Moms because I knew they'd have some wonky reason I was born this way. Whatever. I was just so relieved it was over and I could go home to the more favorable vicissitudes of running a video store.

CHAPTER 34

By the time I got back to the store on Monday morning, I was considered a bit of a hero, or heroine, depending upon who you ask. It seems Linda was keeping Neil abreast of the goings on in Wonderly vis-à-vis the four corpses and my bungled unmasking of the murderer.

My Moms drove back to Briartown with me, settled me in for a full day and a half of sleep, which was interrupted only by some home-made sustenance. They wouldn't let Neil or Marilyn or Sophie come visit. They were in full Florence Nightingale mode.

By six Monday morning I was feeling fidgety and ready to get to the store, but I drove the ladies to the airport for their ten o'clock flight instead. I got a shiver going over that bridge again, knowing where it led me to the last time my tires bounced over that lumpy pavement.

With heavy hearts, once again, we bid one another farewell. When would I next see two of the most beautiful faces I knew? I pondered whether or not to tell the other two beautiful faces, Bogie and Ingrid, what had happened to me in Kentucky. I'd give that more thought.

My mind was made up about what to say to Neil, so the trip from the airport to Annie's Video and Music Hall seemed to take forever.

Marilyn and Sophie were behind the counter when I walked in.

Marilyn came out, lunging at me, "Oh, my God, you were almost killed," she said holding me in a hug.

"And that beautiful woman was a guy? Who would have thought?"

"Certainly not me, or I would have figured it out sooner. She wasn't really a guy. She'd been working toward not being a guy from early childhood. I found out afterward that she was waiting for the surgery that was going to complete the transition once Bucky was the official owner of Wonderly Entertainment. Best laid plans, yada yada."

"How can you even be talking about this, you were almost dead," scolded Sophie. "You have to stop this shit. It's way too scary."

As I thought back about the week that had just passed, it didn't seem real, it seemed like a story I made up. Then the door opened and reality walked in.

I whispered to Marilyn and Sophie, "Can you split? I have to talk to Neil, privately."

They said cheery hellos to Neil and left, ringing the bell on the door. To me it sounded like *the bell tolls for thee*. I knew that meant that death comes to each of us, and this felt like a death of a kind. Because it was.

Neil walked behind the counter and said, "Hey," in his usual way.

"Hey," I answered.

"You don't have to say anything. I can tell what you've decided," he said.

"Can I explain why?" I pleaded.

"You don't have to, what difference would it make? No is no."

"Can we still work together? Will you stay on as my music buyer and right arm?"

"Wow. You thought I'd leave the store, too? Not a chance; I love this place, it's like family to me, and I'll be fine with moving on without you. Well, I won't be fine, but I'll do it."

This was actually far worse in an emotional way than almost being killed by Vivian. This really stunk—it felt like my heart was being ripped out. Is this what I really wanted? But I couldn't see the other way either. *Stuck in the middle <u>without</u> you,* and not a truck around.

EPILOGUE

Four months later...

Life moved on after my sojourn to Kentucky—but without Neil. Even though I did see him almost every day, things weren't the same. Especially when he showed up one evening with his new girlfriend, Luna. She had a safety pin in her cheek.

The full picture of Vivian Ward Henderson's heinous homicides eventually came into focus. I was made privy to much of it by my Wonderly rep, Linda, and my friend, Detective Tom Ward (no relation to the crazed killer).

It seems Vivian's childhood was full of violence and rape, the details of which are too grisly to describe here.

The police did eventually find the bug in room 237. A recording of Bobby Crane's murder had been routed to Dun's office, where he monitored conversations he felt he needed to hear.

Here's how it all went down, as it was revealed in Vivian's and Bucky's trials. Bobby Crane thought Dun was cheating him on the sales of Bare Bottom Babes tapes. Bobby owned a percentage of that part of the business and knew Vivian had the actual numbers. He told her he'd keep the secret of her being transgender if she gave him the truth of the numbers. She killed him instead.

When Bucky realized Vivian had shot Bobby with his mom's antique pistol, which apparently did work, he knew they had to get rid of Bobby's body. The police could trace that bullet easily. The closest place to dispose of him was the distillery. Hence, Bobby Crane's own personal (and I mean personal) vintage of bourbon.

But while Bucky and Vivian were in room 237 at midnight disposing of Bobby's body, Chief Calvin Danvers (per Dun's orders) came to do the same. What else could they do but dispose of Cal, too?

They clocked him over the head, dragged him down the stairs to his truck, drove to Lake Pleasant, and rolled the truck in to where it sank.

How did I know Vivian was Jessica's killer? In *Pretty Woman*, Julia Roberts' character's name was exactly the same as our murderer—Vivian Ward. Once I saw that, I knew Jessica had grabbed that video off a shelf to name her killer … if it came to that. And it did.

I never could figure out why Chief Earl didn't do anything about finding my fingerprints on the PIN pad outside the warehouse. Maybe he'd grown weary of my shenanigans and decided to give it a pass. Or, maybe, he just didn't check out those fingerprints further.

The saddest part of this whole fiasco for me, besides the four deaths, was that beautiful Vivian Ward Henderson was to be incarcerated with men. Life wasn't fair to her at the beginning. Or at the end. But that's life for you.

While struggling for my life in the distillery, I wondered what Sam Spade would have said in similar circumstances. With my mind otherwise engaged, I drew a blank. But given some time to consider it, one of his quotes from *The Maltese Falcon* came to mind. I hope you'll forgive my artistic license. "You're a *bad* man, sister."

I wasn't surprised to learn that Sugar inherited all that was Dun's. She didn't know if she wanted it, and made it clear she certainly didn't want to manage it. She was not the managing type, she was the lounging type. Sugar was still working out who should operate the hotel and the distillery. I'm pretty sure she'd figure that out in short order since, as she said, she's more given to savoring her own time when toil isn't required.

I shouldn't have been surprised that Rob Woodbury was named president of Wonderly Entertainment. But I was. Not that he didn't richly deserve it, but it meant that he would no longer be coming to my store once a month. He did promise that he'd stop in to visit once in a while though.

Oh, lest you forget about the young scalawags who burned a hole in Prancer, let me assure you that I did not. Dylan Applegate turned up the afternoon of my return with his tail between his legs and his piggy bank in tow: a figurative tail and an actual piggy bank. He wouldn't look me in the eye, but told me he was sorry for what the boys had done. He was quick to point out that he hadn't been the one who brought Prancer to his knees, but felt responsible anyway. He gave me his bank as payment. I removed the small cork at the bottom of the pig's belly and spilled out his fiscal guts, counted out ten dollars, and put the rest back in, and handed it back to him. He could have gone to prom in a few years with what was left in his childhood vault. You may think I'm mean to have taken any money, but what I learned from Helen and Em, and what I hope I taught Bogie and Iggy—is that actions have consequences.

Dealing with the loss of Neil to a goth girl wasn't easy. But one day when we were working together and both bent down to retrieve a video, our lips almost touched. We looked at each other with longing. *What is This Thing Called Love?*

ACKNOWLEDGMENTS

At one time, one reared children not for the joy of it or to enter them in beauty contests or soccer tournaments, but so that they could help with the plowing and harvesting of the family crops. Alas, I have no crops here in Cincinnati, but I do have words. Lots of them. And while I hadn't considered it at the time he was born, my son, David Reed, has fulfilled his familial obligation by plowing through my drafts of words and helping me to harvest this story in its current form. And for that I am forever grateful. Thank you, David, I love you.

And a monumental thank you to copy editor Sandy Koppen. I was happy to provide her a diversion during the pandemic, and she was only too happy to take the opportunity to point out so many grammar mistakes. I believe this is what they refer to as a symbiotic relationship.

To my readers Ellen Coughlin, Deb DeNail, Evelyn Greene, Barbara Heyward, David Lehnartz, and Marilyn Mulhern, I deeply appreciate the time and focus you gave me, poring through the book. Not only are these wonderful people great friends – and one delightful brother and sister– but all have keen eyes.

To Rob Eikenbary, without whose memory of the good old days in the video industry this story would have been a sight thinner, I can only say thank you for helping to set the scene-er-ino, my friend. To Chuck Hookey whose recall for certain spacial layouts helped build the murder scene, many thanks. Also, to David Sergenian, attorney-at-law, for his help with some legalese. And Jim Grate for his assistance in all things automotive. Last but not least, my thanks to Bill Clark my computer guru. Heaven only knows where this ms. would be without you.

Speaking of research, a trip to a bourbon distillery and horse farm in Lexington, Kentucky, with Gayle Capretto, Barbara Duncan, and Ann Verdin not only gave me some good ideas, but was a day trip not to be forgotten. But what happens in Lexington, stays in Lexington, or so I'm told. So enough about that.

To retired detective Steve Forester, thank you again for helping to make the more sordid details of the mystery actually sordid and not preposterous.

And to all my family and friends who have supported me with love, encouragement, and the occasional much needed kick in the pants, my gratitude knows no end.